Listening to the Rain

Miriam Thor

I0690158

All scripture quotations, unless otherwise indicated, are taken from the Holy Bible, New International Version(R), NIV(R), Copyright 1973, 1978, 1984, 2011 by Biblica, Inc.™ Used by permission of Zondervan. All rights reserved worldwide. www.zondervan.com

Scripture quotations, marked KJV are taken from the King James translation, public domain. Scripture quotations marked DR, are taken from the Douay Rheims translation, public domain.

Scripture texts marked NAB are taken from the *New American Bible, revised edition* Copyright 2010, 1991, 1986, 1970 Confraternity of Christian Doctrine, Washington, D.C. and are used by permission of the copyright owner. All Rights Reserved. No part of the New American Bible may be reproduced in any form without permission in writing from the copyright owner.

Cover Art by *Nicola Martinez*

Watershed Books, a division of Pelican Ventures, LLC
www.pelicanbookgroup.com PO Box 1738 *Aztec, NM * 87410
Watershed Books praise and splash logo is a trademark of Pelican Ventures, LLC

Publishing History
First Watershed Edition, 2022
Paperback Edition ISBN 978-1-5223-0498-2
Published in the United States of America

Dedication

To Hannah, Hannahmae, and Mrs. Nancy. Your feedback helped make the book what it is today.

What People are Saying

"I loved this book! It left me feeling hopeful and nostalgic for my family. Ally and her cousins are such amazing characters. Their bond draws you in with complete sincerity and humanity. And their experience reminds me that we all take a journey to learn new things about ourselves and the people we love."

- Dr. Hannah Mayfield.

PROLOGUE

~March 30, 2019; 3:30 p.m.~

Beep…Beep…Beep…

A heart monitor. My grandpa's heart monitor. That and the rain pattering against the window are the only sounds I've heard in the last hour. I'm sitting in one of those hospital chairs that looks comfortable until you actually have to sit in it. There's a microbiology textbook open in my lap, and I should be studying for my test next week. I need a good grade in this class if I want to keep my GPA high enough to get into medical school and become an audiologist. Despite knowing all of that, I'm not studying. I can't.

Not here. Not now.

Instead, I'm staring at Grandpa's face and praying God will give him the strength to get through this.

Sitting in this hospital room certainly does bring back memories. This is the only hospital in our parish, so any time one of us was hurt or sick, we came here. We came for a lot of minor things like stitches and broken bones. A few of the nurses in the emergency room knew my whole family by name, and they always gave us candy when we left. Those visits weren't so bad.

But there was one visit that wasn't like that at all, that I can't think about without a twinge of pain even now. No, I don't want to think about that.

Not here. Not now.

Less painful memories would make a better distraction anyway. Let's see. Maybe my ballet recital during freshman year...that was the beginning of something interesting.

1

— TUTUS AND TATTERS

~December 19, 2014~

Biting my lip, I looked down at my red and white costume. This really wasn't how I'd pictured myself at my first ballet recital. When I'd signed up for lessons a few months ago, I'd envisioned myself wearing a leotard with a flowing skirt, my brown hair tucked into a neat bun. But no, our instructor, Madame Clarisse, insisted that all the beginning ballerinas had to be candy canes for the Christmas recital. The bulky costume was doing nothing to help my nerves.

As I took my place in line, I pretended it wasn't embarrassing to be so much taller than the other candy canes. My classmates were all under the age of eight. Apparently, fourteen was an awkward age to begin ballet. I wished Missy would have mentioned that before I signed up.

Standing in line, my hands shook. Would ballet be *my thing*? The talent that would bring people to their feet and make them think I was exceptional? In the next hour, I would know one way or the other. I both looked forward to and dreaded the answer.

Please, Lord, I prayed. *Help me do well in the recital. Please let ballet be my thing.*

When the music started, I tiptoed to my assigned spot. The candy canes were arranged in a semi-circle along the back and sides of the stage. Unfortunately, as the tallest, I had to stand at the back. I'd tried to convince Madame Clarisse that I wouldn't block any of the other dancers if she placed me on the far-left or right side, but she hadn't listened.

As I spun and swayed to the first song, I saw Missy leaping along the front of the stage in her fairy costume with her auburn hair fixed in a French braid. Since Missy was an advanced student, she got to move around a lot more than I did. Despite knowing how much she deserved it, I couldn't help but feel a bit jealous.

Pushing that thought aside, I searched the audience for my family, but it was too dark to find them. The few faces I could see in the crowd appeared bored, and none of them were looking at me. It was as if I was invisible.

During the second song, one of the little candy canes next to me fell down. When I stepped out of place to help her up, I bumped one of the ornaments twirling in front of me, and she almost fell over. She caught herself and kept going as though nothing had happened. It was a minor mishap, but it really shook my confidence. If I could make a mistake as a candy cane in the back row, chances were that ballet wasn't going to be my thing.

The rest of the recital went smoothly, but by the end, I was tired, sweaty, and wondering why I had let Missy talk me into this. After I changed out of my costume, I walked to where the audience had been sitting and found Grandpa and my cousins standing in one of the aisles near the back.

"Great job, Ally," Grandpa told me, his mouth curving in a smile beneath his gray mustache.

"You were a really good candy cane," James said.

When I raised my eyebrows, Billy nodded in confirmation.

"Thanks," I said, feeling a little better.

"You ready to go?" Billy asked. "I'm hungry."

I bit back a laugh. Billy was always hungry.

"Give me just a minute," I said. "I want to wish Missy and her mom a merry Christmas."

"Couldn't you have told her that on the bus this afternoon?" Billy asked, only half-joking.

Before I could respond, Grandpa said, "We'll go out to the car. Ally, you can join us after you find Missy."

"Thanks, Grandpa," I said and started scanning the crowd.

After a moment, I spotted Missy and took a step toward her.

"So, how did it feel to be the only candy cane over four feet tall?" someone behind me asked.

Cringing, I turned to face Jenny, my least favorite person in all of Mayville. Tonight, her perfect blonde hair was held back with a red headband.

"What are you doing here?" I demanded.

"My little sister was the ornament you almost knocked over with your clumsy feet," she said. "Fortunately, Claire is more graceful than you, or it could have been a disaster."

I clenched my teeth, knowing it was true. Stepping out of line to help the little candy cane had been a mistake, one that could have been more costly than it was.

"Don't you have anything better to do right now?" I demanded, half-expecting her to say no. Tormenting me seemed to be one of her favorite pastimes.

"You're right, I do," she said, starting to turn away. "I mean, if you want to make a fool of yourself by spinning around like a monkey in a tutu, who am I to stop you?"

With that parting jibe, she walked away. Biting the inside of my cheek, I blinked back my tears. Jenny had hated me since I'd attempted to show her my pet spider in second grade, and she had gone out of her way to make my life miserable ever since. Most of the time, I didn't let her get to me anymore, but tonight, she'd touched a nerve.

Trying not to feel despondent, I glanced around the room again and caught sight of Missy and her mom walking toward the back door. Pasting a smile on my face, I hurried over to them.

"Great job in the recital, Missy," I said. "You made a fantastic fairy."

She grinned. "Thanks. You were a great candy cane, too. I watched you whenever I could."

Which probably wasn't often considering how much she'd been moving around. I decided not to point that out.

"You both did wonderful," Ms. Cathy said.

"Thank you," I said, pretending I believed her. "Well, Grandpa's waiting for me, but I wanted to wish you both a merry Christmas."

"Merry Christmas to you too," Missy replied.

"Yes," Ms. Cathy said. "And tell your grandpa and cousins merry Christmas as well."

"I will," I said and walked out to the car.

As usual when we were in the car together, Billy was riding shotgun, so I climbed into the backseat with James.

About halfway home, James leaned toward me. It was so dark that I could barely see his short brown hair, much less his facial expression, but I knew his gray eyes were filled with concern.

"You OK?" he whispered, so that only I could hear.

I shrugged. "I had a little run in with Jenny."

James sighed. "The candy canes really did add a lot to the show, Ally. And you were an important part of that. Don't worry about Jenny's opinion. She would have found something bad to say no matter what. She always does."

"Yeah, you're right," I said, wishing it helped.

I hadn't been as bad as Jenny claimed, but I hadn't been great either. Which meant my hopes for ballet being my thing were now in tatters. I would stick it out until the end of the year, only because Grandpa insisted that we not break our commitments, but I'd have to find something else to be my thing.

I heaved a sigh. Billy had been the best player on every sports team he'd ever joined, and James was an awesome musician. People had cheered for them so many times I'd lost count. But despite trying band, choir, and every sport I could think of, I had yet to find something I was really good at. I hadn't had a lot of hope that ballet would be my thing, but after looking through the sports and extra-curriculars at Mayville High, it had seemed like the best option. Now, I'd have to start looking again.

"Don't look so glum, Ally," Billy said, his blond hair bouncing against his forehead as he turned to look at me. "It's Christmas break."

Not wanting to bring down my entire family's mood, I hitched a smile on my face.

"Yep," I said. "Two weeks with no school. What else could we need?"

Billy nodded like that settled the matter and turned back to face the front.

James gave me a sideways look that said he didn't buy my act for a second. A look I pointedly ignored.

"Let's listen to Christmas music," I said.

Grandpa nodded and turned on the radio.

When we got home, we had leftover spaghetti for dinner. As I ate, I surveyed the kitchen's white tile floors and countertops. Somehow, they were already getting dingy, even though it had been less than a week since I'd scrubbed them. How was that even possible? Shaking my head, I turned my attention back to my food.

When we were all finished eating, Grandpa asked, "Whose turn is it to wash the dishes?"

"Mine," Billy and I said in unison. All four of us

took turns doing the dishes, two at a time, so one could wash while the other dried.

"Good," Grandpa said. "I'll go ahead and take a shower."

He stood and brought his dishes to the sink. The rest of us did the same. As James grabbed a book and headed to the porch, Billy and I played Rock Paper Scissors to see which task we would do. I won, so I dried and put away each dish after Billy washed it. We finished just as Grandpa got out of the shower.

"Good timing," I said and grabbed my pajamas from my room before heading to take a shower.

When I finished, I found Billy in his and James's room and told him it was his turn in the bathroom. After he showered, he'd let James know it was his turn, just as he did every night.

When we were all clean, Grandpa called us to the living room to pray. I'd been in my room reading, but I came quickly when he called. For reasons I couldn't quite put into words, this was one of my favorite parts of the day.

Grandpa was already kneeling on the floor, so I knelt on his right. When my cousins joined us, Billy knelt across from me, and James knelt across from Grandpa. It was as close to a circle as we could make with four people, and we knelt in that exact formation every night. Grandpa prayed first, and we worked our way around the circle. Billy first, James second, me last. It worked out well. Grandpa and James tended to say long prayers, while Billy and I both said short ones. So we alternated between long and short. Once I said amen, we told each other good night and headed to bed.

After closing the door, I surveyed my room, my favorite place in the house. The light pink walls and the patchwork quilt my grandma made helped it feel cozy, despite how worn the white furniture looked.

Since I wasn't quite ready to go to sleep, I rested on my bed and read a few more chapters of my book. Then I got up and turned off the light. Since Grandpa insisted my room stay neat, it was easy to find my way back to my bed in the dark. As I snuggled under the quilt, I decided to pray for what I wanted most but had been unwilling to say in front of my family.

Lord, please help me find my thing. Something I'm really good at, that will make people cheer just for me.

Feeling better now that I'd shared my deepest desire with the Lord, I drifted off to sleep.

2

—A New Teacher and New Idea

"Rise and shine, Ally," Grandpa said, turning on the light in my bedroom. "It's time to get ready for school."

With a groan, I pulled my quilt over my head, wondering how Christmas break could possibly be over already. For a few minutes, I just lay there, contemplating what would happen if I simply refused to get out of bed. Picturing Grandpa's reaction had me on my feet and heading to the chicken coop in a matter of seconds.

After I gathered eggs, I ate breakfast and got ready as quickly as I could. Once I was dressed, I surveyed myself in the full-length mirror on the back of my bedroom door. Even though it was winter, my skin was fairly tan. And I'd left my brown hair down, so the tips just brushed my shoulders. My eyes, the spitting image of Grandpa's green ones, stared back at me, filled with determination.

"I will find my thing," I told my reflection. "I won't give up, no matter what."

Satisfied, I grabbed my backpack and headed to the living room to wait for my cousins. As I sank down on the purple, velvet couch, I couldn't help but wish we had cable. Or satellite. Or internet. Over break, I'd tried again to convince Grandpa that we should get some sort of technology from this millennium. He'd said it was a waste of money and that if the "bunny ear" antenna had been good enough for his children, they were good enough for us.

When my cousins were finally ready, the three of us headed to the kitchen for inspection. Grandpa looked us over carefully, just as he did every day before we left for school. I'd learned a long time ago what he was looking for. As a man who wore overalls every day, Grandpa didn't care if we looked cool or pretty. But as a former Marine drill sergeant, he cared if we looked neat.

"You all look great," he said after a moment. "I hope you have a good day."

He patted each of us on the back as we went out the door. It was a fifteen-minute walk to the end of our road, past a lot of soy beans and two houses that belonged to our only neighbors, Mr. Codwaller and Mr. Francis. We walked to the end of the road and waited for the bus. The drive to school would take thirty minutes. When the bus pulled up, I immediately went to sit with Missy.

"Hey, Ally," she said. "How was your break?"

"Pretty good," I replied. "How about you?"

"It was fine," she said, her hazel eyes downcast.

Frowning, I studied my best friend. She always had a fair complexion, but today, her skin was as white as chalk.

"You OK?" I asked.

She shrugged one shoulder. "Yeah. It's just…we're getting a new English teacher today."

Right. Now that I thought about it, Mrs. Cloverfield had mentioned she was retiring right before break. Between the recital and Christmas, I'd forgotten all about it. Clearly, Missy hadn't.

"It'll be fine," I told her.

"I'm sure you're right," Missy said, though she didn't sound sure at all.

I pursed my lips, unsure what to say. Missy's dyslexia had always made English class difficult for her, especially when other students, and even a few teachers, had given her a hard time about it. I was trying to think of a way to cheer her up when someone sat down in the seat behind us.

"I'm sorry to interrupt, but you're Ally, right?"

I turned around to see Tyler Ferguson, a sophomore with curly black hair and a slight overbite. Since we went to the same church, I was pretty sure he knew my name, which meant he was just trying to make conversation. I had no problem with that.

"Yep, that's me," I said with a smile. "And you're Tyler."

He nodded. "I know we've seen each other around, but I don't think we've ever officially introduced ourselves, and I'd like to get to know you."

I tried to hide my surprise. Was this guy actually flirting with me? I'd hoped that guys would start to take an interest in me when I started high school, but this was the first time it had happened.

"Hi, Tyler," Billy said, appearing out of nowhere

and dropping into the seat next to him. "Long time, no see."

"Hi, Billy," Tyler said, obviously uncomfortable.

I narrowed my eyes at Billy, hoping he would take the hint and go away. He ignored me.

"Listen, Tyler," Billy said. "You seem like a nice enough guy, but if I see you talking to my cousin again…you'll regret it."

He held up his fist to emphasize his point, and all the blood drained from Tyler's face. Billy was the captain of the football team, and his muscles weren't just for show.

"Billy, what are you doing?" I demanded.

"Protecting you," he said, gaze still on Tyler.

"I don't need protecting," I snapped, glaring at him.

"What's going on?" James asked.

I jumped. I'd been so focused on Billy's outrageous behavior that I hadn't noticed my other cousin walk up and sit behind Billy. When I looked at him, I felt relief wash over me. James would have some sense.

"Billy's threatening to kill Tyler if he even looks at me," I told him.

"I won't kill him," Billy said. "I'll just take him to the back of the bus and beat him to a pulp."

James shook his head. "You can't do that."

I smiled smugly at Billy, who took his gaze off Tyler for the first time to frown at James.

"You want him going out with Ally?" he asked, a note of disbelief in his voice.

"Of course not," James said. "But you can't beat

him up here. You'll be suspended. Wait until you're at church or something, and then beat him to a pulp."

Billy nodded. "Good point."

He looked at Tyler with a smile that bared more teeth than usual. "Spread the word. Anyone who wants to go out with Ally has to go through me first."

I glared at my cousins, wishing I wouldn't get suspended for punching them. They ignored me and walked off together, looking quite pleased with themselves.

"Tyler," I said desperately.

"Later, Ally." He moved to a different seat without looking at me.

"They're unbelievable." I turned to face the front of the bus.

"I'm sure they have your best interest at heart," Missy said with a shrug.

"Yeah, if what's in my best interest is not having a boyfriend until I'm thirty."

"It's kind of sweet that they want to protect you," she added.

I rolled my eyes. Missy always did her best to give people the benefit of the doubt. Usually I didn't mind, but in this case, it was a bit annoying. Before I could tell her so, the bus pulled into the school parking lot, and we walked to the gym to wait. We'd barely set foot inside it when the bell rang, sending us to our homeroom class.

When Missy and I reached Mrs. Cloverfield's old classroom, we found our new teacher waiting outside the door. She was thin with black hair and looked about the same age as Missy's mom.

"Good morning," she said, smiling at us as we approached her. "Please go in and find your seat."

When we entered the classroom, I thought I might be blinded by the bright posters she'd added to the walls. The desks were still in rows, but now each one had a nametag taped to it. Feeling as if I'd gone back to elementary school, I walked around until I found the one labeled "Kallyna Griffin." As I sat down, I looked around and was disappointed to find that Missy's seat was on the other side of the room. Then I noticed Jenny's was, too. That was something, at least.

When the bell rang, the teacher came in and shut the door.

"Good morning, class," she said with a bright smile. "My name is Mrs. Chamberlain, and I'll be your English teacher for the rest of this year. Now, before we get started, I want to see who's here." She grabbed a clipboard from her desk. "Raise your hand when I call your name. If I say your name wrong or if you go by a different name, please let me know."

As she read off names, I got ready to help her when she got to mine. Teachers always struggled to pronounce it correctly.

"Tommy Goins?" Mrs. Chamberlain said. A boy with hair so short you couldn't tell what color it was raised his hand.

"Ka...lie..." she began.

"Kuh-leena," I said, "but you can call me Ally."

"Ally?" she asked, puzzled. "Why not Kally?"

I did my best not to sigh. Just once, it would be

nice if a teacher could accept my nickname without questioning it.

"When I was born, my older brother, Jason, was two," I explained. "When he tried to say Kally, it sounded like Ally, and the name just stuck."

That was what Grandpa had told me. Obviously, I couldn't remember that far back. I couldn't even remember Jason.

"Ally, it is," Mrs. Chamberlain said and continued with the roll.

When she finished, she introduced the short story we would be studying that week. Overall, she seemed like a run-of-the-mill teacher: not too strict, not too interesting, but nice enough. I figured her class would be pretty easy.

When there were about ten minutes left in class, Mrs. Chamberlain said she wanted to get to know us better and asked us to each tell a little about ourselves: what subject we liked best, if we played any sports, how many siblings we had, etc. As soon as she finished explaining what to do, I braced myself. I hadn't expected to have to tell this story today.

I didn't really pay attention while most of the other students spoke, though I did catch a few random facts. Apparently, Johnny liked to draw, Sarah had four cats, and Jacob liked to go fishing. I did smile encouragingly at Missy as she whispered that she was an only child and liked to do ballet. Half of the class probably didn't hear her, but Mrs. Chamberlain didn't seem to care. By the time my turn came, my stomach was in knots, but I did my best not to show it.

"OK, Ally," Mrs. Chamberlain said, "you're up."

I took a deep breath. "My name is Ally Griffin, and I like to read."

Mrs. Chamberlain nodded. "And what about your family? Is Jason your only brother?"

"Actually, Jason died in a car accident with my parents when I was a baby," I replied, careful to keep my voice even. "I live with my grandpa and two cousins now."

"Your cousins live there too?" Mrs. Chamberlain asked, her wide eyes filling with tears that she did her best to blink away.

"Yeah," I replied stonily. "Billy's family died in the same accident as mine. They'd gone to the movies, and got hit by an eighteen-wheeler on the way home. James's mom died giving birth to his little sister, and his dad and sister drowned a few years later."

That might have been more information than she wanted to know, but I figured it was best to get it all out of the way.

"I'm so sorry," Mrs. Chamberlain murmured. She sniffed and quickly turned to the next student. "What about you, Tammie?"

As the girl across from me started talking about her hobbies, I did my best not to roll my eyes. Teachers always reacted that way to hearing about my family, as though it was the saddest thing they'd ever heard. It really got on my nerves. I loved Grandpa and my cousins dearly, and even though I would have liked to have known my parents and brother, I didn't feel as if my life had been that tragic. But teachers never seemed to understand that.

When the bell finally rang, I was glad to put Mrs. Chamberlain's class behind me. The rest of the day was pretty normal until I got to physical science, my first class after lunch.

"Good afternoon," Mrs. Mason said. "I hope you had a good break. Before we get started, I have an announcement to make. In a few weeks, our school will be having a talent show. All students are eligible to participate, and there will be prizes for the first, second, and third place winners. If you're interested in participating, please let me know. You have to sign up by this Friday."

She pointed to a poster advertising the talent show on her bulletin board and then started teaching a lesson about the periodic table. I tuned her out, my mind spinning. A talent show? This could be exactly what I'd been looking for.

I loved to sing, and Grandpa had always told me I had a nice voice. My stint in the children's choir at church had gone better than most of the activities I'd tried. I'd thought it couldn't be my thing because there was no way to stand out from the rest of the group. Singing by myself would eliminate that problem. And if I won, everyone would cheer and congratulate me. Why hadn't I thought of this before?

By the end of class, I couldn't have told someone the difference between hydrogen and helium if my life depended on it, but I knew one thing for sure: I planned to sing in the talent show.

3

—THE "TALENT" SHOW?

When we got on the bus that afternoon, I couldn't wait to share my good news with Missy.

"Wasn't Mrs. Mason's announcement exciting?" I asked as soon as we sat down.

Missy gave me a blank look. "What announcement?"

I stared at her incredulously. How could she have forgotten something so important?

"About the talent show," I explained, trying not to sound impatient.

"Oh," Missy said, unenthused. "I guess. It should give us some time out of class. That'll be nice."

"It's way more exciting than that," I told her, shaking my head. "Guess who's going to enter?"

She thought for a second. "James?"

I glared at her. "No. Me. Why would you think James is entering?"

Missy looked at the floor. "I don't know. You told me about him getting that guitar for his birthday, and his singing is…nice." She paused before adding, "But you entering is a great idea, too."

I frowned. Missy was acting kind of weird, but she had a point. James had a beautiful voice, though he seldom sang for an audience. I always tried to sit next to him at church, so I could hear him sing. He also played the keyboard in our youth group's praise band, the clarinet in the marching band, and thanks to Grandpa's birthday gift, was learning to play the guitar. Music was his thing. Just like baseball and football were Billy's thing.

I really hoped the talent show could be an opportunity for me to shine...but only if James didn't enter. Competing against my cousin was unthinkable. Before I got too excited, I had to ask him if he planned to participate. I decided to discuss it with him as soon as we got off the bus. Since Billy had baseball practice, it would be the perfect opportunity for us to talk, just the two of us.

Unfortunately, it started raining a few minutes before the bus reached our stop. By unspoken consent, the two of us walked home as quickly as we could so that we could get warm and dry as soon as possible.

I wanted to talk to James as soon as I'd changed into dry clothes, but I knew better than to try. Grandpa insisted that we start on our homework as soon as we got home, and while I was willing to bend that rule from time to time, James definitely was not. Resigned to wait, I solved a page of equations and read the short story Mrs. Chamberlain had assigned.

When I was finished, I went in search of my cousin to see if he had completed his homework, too. I found him sitting in a rocking chair on the porch with his eyes closed.

"What are you doing?" I asked, puzzled.

He opened his eyes and looked at me. "Listening to the rain. God plays beautiful music, don't you think?"

I wasn't sure how to respond. James said stuff like that sometimes. Random, weird stuff. And I was never sure what to make of it.

"It's not music, James," I said. "It's just water hitting the roof."

He shrugged, unperturbed, and studied my face. "What's wrong, Ally?"

"What makes you think something's wrong?" I demanded.

"You've got that 'I really want to ask you something, but I don't know how you'll take it' look on your face."

I smiled. He always could read me like an open book.

"Well..." I said slowly. "You heard about the talent show at school today, right?"

He nodded. "Yeah, Mr. Jenkins announced it in homeroom."

I bit my lip and stared at my lap. I wanted to sing in the talent show so badly. What if James did, too?

"What about it?" James prompted when I didn't continue.

"Do you want to enter?" I asked and held my breath.

"No," he said. "Performing in front of all the kids at school and a panel of judges doesn't sound like much fun to me."

I heaved a sigh of relief and grinned at him.

"Good."

"Does that smile mean you plan on entering?" he asked.

"Yep," I said. "I didn't want to compete against you, though."

He smiled. "So, what will you sing?"

I didn't even ask how he knew I planned to sing. We both knew my talents. Unless I wanted to bring our hens to roost on the stage and gather their eggs, singing was my only real option.

"I don't know yet," I said, "but I'll figure it out." I started to turn around. "You can go back to your...rain listening now."

He rolled his eyes as I headed back inside.

When I signed up for the talent show the next day at school, Mrs. Mason told me I would need to provide a CD with any music I would need. Fortunately for me, Missy's mom had an online shopping account with next-day shipping and infinite understanding when it came to my lack of technology. Once I chose a song, all I had to do was give Missy the money I'd saved from my last birthday, and Ms. Cathy took care of the rest.

After the CD arrived, I had to rehearse. And I did. Every spare minute I had. While I was getting ready for school, walking to the bus stop, walking home from the bus stop, doing chores, taking a shower...I'm pretty sure my whole family was sick of that song by the end of the first day. By the time the talent show came around, they were probably ready to murder the person who wrote it. I didn't care. I had to be ready.

James helped me a lot. He was the only one in my

family with the patience to willingly listen to that song as many times as I asked. He even convinced Grandpa to ask Pastor Benjamin to let me practice in the church sanctuary with a microphone. When the day of the talent show finally arrived, I knew I was ready.

That morning, I got up an hour early. After gathering eggs and gobbling my breakfast, I braided my hair and put on the plaid top, blue jean skirt, and boots I'd picked out days before. After checking myself in the mirror one last time, I headed to the living room and discovered it would be fifteen minutes before my cousins even got up. I stared at the cuckoo clock in despair. How would I ever wait over an hour for them to get ready? With a sigh, I went to my room to grab a book.

An eternity later, Billy and James were finally ready to leave. After Grandpa inspected us and offered encouragement for my performance, I walked to the bus stop so fast that I was breathing heavily when I got there. Billy and James, who didn't share my urgency, arrived several minutes later.

"Look, James," Billy said in mock astonishment, "the bus isn't here yet. Ally sprinting to get here didn't make it arrive any sooner."

James smiled sleepily, but I stuck my tongue out at Billy.

"Don't give me a hard time. I'm nervous enough."

"I hadn't noticed," Billy said dryly. Then, his tone softened. "You'll do great, Ally. You've got a beautiful voice, and you've *definitely* practiced enough."

"Thanks, Billy," I said as the bus pulled up.

I'm not sure how I got through my classes that day. Mrs. Mason gave us a quiz on the periodic table, and my other teachers tried valiantly to teach me about quadratic equations, the Renaissance, and the theme of the short story we read. I didn't absorb a word of it. Instead of paying attention, I fidgeted, replayed the song in my mind, and even wrote out the lyrics. I wanted to win the talent show so badly. I was sure that if I won, singing for an audience could be my thing. Granted, it would be similar to James's thing but not exactly the same.

After lunch, a teacher made an all-call for the talent show contestants to report to the auditorium. When we arrived, they told us the order in which we'd be performing. There were nineteen contestants, and I was number ten, exactly in the middle. I wasn't sure if that was a good or a bad thing. It was better than being first or last, but it might make me easier for the judges to forget. Since it couldn't be helped, I did my best not to worry about it.

After we received our instructions, we went to wait backstage as the student body filed into the auditorium. Knowing that would take a while, I tried to find something to pass the time. First, I looked around the narrow hallway where we were standing. It was to the left of the stage with bare white walls and a tile floor. No help there. Then I decided to talk to the other contestants. I spotted Johnny sitting near the curtain, sketchbook in hand, so I walked over to him.

"What are you doing for your talent?" I asked.

He glanced around nervously as if he expected to

find Billy lurking around the corner, waiting to pounce.

"Drawing," he said, without meeting my gaze.

I raised my eyebrows. How did he plan to draw for an audience? Given the slightly green tinge of his cheeks, I decided not to ask. "That's cool."

After he shrugged one shoulder, I gritted my teeth and imagined wringing Billy's neck for making all the guys at school afraid to talk to me. Then I remembered his compliment that morning and decided that I didn't really want to strangle him. Much.

I tried talking to a few other contestants, but no one really wanted to chat. With no one to talk to, I decided to pray instead. At least God wouldn't glare at me or tell me to leave Him alone.

Please let me win, God. It would mean a lot to me.

Deep down, I knew God might not care if I won the talent show. He might even think not winning would help build character. Still, it never hurt to ask.

At long last—thirty minutes—the talent show began. Mr. Demmings, our principal, made a few announcements and then introduced the first contestant, a tenth-grade girl named Larissa who did an interpretive dance...with no music. We could only see part of what she did from backstage, but she seemed to just run around jumping and swinging her arms, looking like a monkey who'd had too much caffeine. I tried not to look at her as if she was weird when she came backstage, but I'm not sure if I succeeded. Still, I knew I would definitely beat her, and that only left eighteen more contestants to go.

Maybe they would all do interpretive dances. Then I would win for sure.

Johnny was second. He brought his sketchbook on stage, sat down, and drew for ten minutes without saying a word. Then, he silently turned the picture around for everyone to see. He'd drawn our school mascot, a buzzard, which might be one of the worst mascots in history. He'd even drawn a decaying deer carcass for it to eat. I'd like to say our football team was about to play the Bucks, so at least that would've symbolized something. Sadly, that wasn't the case.

After he showed his picture, Johnny walked backstage, looking pleased with himself. I decided maybe his refusing to talk to me was a good thing. That deer carcass looked very realistic.

The third contestant twirled a baton and dropped it at least ten times. The baton spent as much time on the stage as it did in her hand. As she walked backstage looking proud of herself, I decided maybe winning would be easier than I thought.

The fourth contestant attempted to sing, but she had a cold and could barely get a sound out. Halfway through the song, she had a coughing fit and had to stop. I tried really hard to feel bad for her and almost succeeded.

The fifth contestant did a dramatic declaiming of a poem. I shook my head and decided she'd watched one too many historical dramas. That was the only way she could have thought it was a good idea. Sure, declaiming worked for heroines at concerts in the nineteenth century, but their audience was not a room full of high schoolers who appreciated poetry as much a cat appreciates being thrown in a lake.

The sixth contestant did pig calls. Loud, high-pitched pig calls. Resisting the urge to cover my ears, I started to wonder if most high schoolers were familiar with the definition of the word *talent*.

The seventh contestant did impersonations of the teachers and staff. He was pretty funny, or at least the students thought so. Mr. Demmings interrupted him halfway through and announced that he was disqualified. As the two of them walked backstage, I heard Mr. Demmings tell him to come to his office as soon as the talent show was over.

The eighth contestant performed a song using sign language, and the ninth did a tap dance. They both seemed to do all right, but since I didn't know sign language and wasn't great at dancing, it was hard to know for sure. Still, I would've preferred to follow the pig calls. I would've sounded great by contrast.

When the announcer called for contestant ten, I took a deep breath and walked onstage. I grabbed the microphone and held it tightly in my sweaty hands while I looked around at the assembled students. There were a lot of them. As my music started to play, I glanced at some of their faces, forcing myself to breathe. I saw Missy smiling encouragingly, and then I saw Jenny a few rows behind her. She had a truly evil look on her face, as if she expected me to fail and was ready to enjoy it. I tried to swallow, but my throat was too dry. The lights shone in my eyes, and sweat trickled down my back.

When the music got to the place where I was supposed to start singing, I took a deep breath and opened my lips, but no sound came out. After a couple seconds, I tried again. Nothing. I stared at the crowd, unsure what to do. I just stood there, my mouth working like a fish fresh out of the water until the horror of the situation finally penetrated my slow-moving brain. Then I turned and ran off the stage.

I raced past the other contestants without looking at them and turned a corner at the end of the hall. I saw several doors and opened the first one, which was labeled "Prop Room." I ran in, slammed the door behind me, and collapsed onto my knees. Silent sobs shook my whole body. It was worse than I could have imagined. Even Larissa and her "dance" were better than me. I couldn't believe I froze. After all that practice, I *froze*. I would never get over the humiliation. Jenny would make sure of it. In the midst of my swirling thoughts, I heard a knock on the door.

"Go away!" I screamed. No one could see me like this. No one.

The door opened. I glanced up and through my tears saw brown hair, a red t-shirt, and jeans. James. He knelt down beside me.

"It's OK, Ally," he said, putting an arm around my shoulders. "It's OK."

I resisted for a second and then let him pull me into a hug. I cried against his shoulder, getting snot and saltwater all over his favorite t-shirt. He didn't budge. After a minute, I pulled away from him.

"It's not OK. I froze, James. I made an idiot out of

myself."

He shook his head. "A lot of people get stage fright. It's nothing to be ashamed of."

I swallowed hard, wanting to make him understand. "I will never be able to live this down. Jenny will make sure no one ever forgets it."

James sighed. "Forget about Jenny. She's just a bad egg. No one else will think any worse of you. Not in the long run anyway."

I shook my head. He still didn't understand.

"But this was my chance, James," I said. "My chance to be really good at something, just like you and Billy."

He frowned as if I wasn't making sense.

"Billy has baseball and football," I explained. "And you have your instruments, but I don't have anything. I—"

"That's not true, Ally," he said. "You've done a lot of things: dance, softball, soccer, piano."

"But I haven't been good at them," I said, trying not to sound pathetic.

"You haven't given yourself a chance to be good at them," he said. "You did each one for a year or less. I didn't play the piano well after a year, and I certainly haven't mastered the guitar in the last few months. Don't be so hard on yourself."

I noticed James didn't mention Billy at all, which made sense. Billy had been the best player on every baseball team he'd ever joined. He had also been good at football since the day he'd tried out for the team. His arms were strong from working in the garden, and he was naturally athletic. They'd made him the quarterback of the middle school team after just a month. I decided not to mention any of that to James since he was trying so hard to comfort me. Besides, he already knew.

"Billy is the exception, not the rule," James said, reading my mind as usual.

"I know," I said. "I just want to be good at something."

"You're good at a lot of things," he said. "You're good at being kind to people and standing up for yourself and your friends. You can shell every vegetable known to man, and you gather eggs faster than anyone I know." He smiled, and I managed a shaky smile of my own. There was too much truth in that to ignore.

"Now, do you still want to perform?" he asked.

I frowned. "It's too late. I missed my chance."

"No, it's not," he said. "I talked to Mr. Demmings on my way back here. He said you could try again after all the contestants are finished."

I felt a flicker of hope but quickly snuffed it out.

"I can't, James. I'll freeze again. I know it. I'll look at the lights and the people, and—"

"So, don't look at the lights and the people," he said. "Look at me. I'll come right near the front, and you can sing to me. I know you can do that. You've done it at least a hundred times in the last week."

I laughed weakly. It was true.

"Maybe I could do that."

"Only if you want to," he said. "I don't care one

way or the other, but I think you'll be disappointed in yourself if you don't try again."

I nodded, knowing he was right.

"OK," he said. "Go to the bathroom and splash some water on your face. I'll tell Mr. Demmings."

He stood up and helped me to my feet.

As we left the prop room, I said, "James."

He turned back to look at me.

"Thanks."

He patted me on the arm. "Any time," he said and went to find the principal.

I washed my face and went back to stand with the other contestants. I couldn't bring myself to meet their eyes, so I turned my attention to the stage. The eighteenth contestant was attempting to yodel. My lips quirked, and I stifled a laugh. Most high schoolers truly didn't understand the definition of *talent*, did they?

The nineteenth contestant burped the Pledge of Allegiance, and I closed my eyes in horror. Why didn't someone screen these acts before letting us perform them? At least following him was better than following the tap dance.

"Let's hear it again for contestant ten," the announcer said once the burper had left the stage.

Taking a deep breath, I walked onstage. It was all just like before. The crowd. The lights. I heard a snicker from about where Jenny had been sitting but did my best to ignore it. I walked to the microphone and pulled it off the stand. When the music started, I searched the crowd for James.

He was there, just as he said he'd be, kneeling in the center aisle near the front row. His gaze held encouragement and confidence. He knew I could do this.

When the CD got to the end of the intro music, I stared directly at him and sang.

I kept my eyes fixed on James through the entire first verse. Then I started to get a little more confident. I had sung this a million times, after all. I risked looking at the crowd and found that I could. My gaze swept over the students, the judges, and even Jenny. As I finished the song and the music faded, the crowd applauded. It was a wonderful feeling, knowing they enjoyed hearing me sing. As I walked backstage, I knew I would win.

I didn't. But I got second place. I won a red ribbon, a homework pass, and a pack of scented markers. Not a bad prize at all. Melinda Bates, the eighth contestant who had signed the song, won first place. As much as I wanted to, I couldn't begrudge it to her. There had been something beautiful about her signs, and she seemed like a sweet girl. Besides, second place gave me enough bragging rights to shut up Jenny whenever she brought up my initial attempt to perform.

That night at home, Grandpa put my ribbon on display on the piano, right next to Billy's football MVP trophy. He also made crawfish ètouffèe, a spicy Cajun dish served over rice, as a treat for supper. After he said the blessing, Grandpa asked me to tell him all about the talent show. He'd wanted to come, but he'd had to go to an appointment with his cardiologist that had been scheduled for months.

As I ate, I told him everything I could remember, including some of the more unusual "talents." Billy filled in everything I forgot. When I got to the part where I froze and ran off the stage, Grandpa was shocked.

"How did you win second place if you didn't sing?" he asked.

"The other acts were so bad that she won by doing nothing," Billy said, a teasing note in his voice.

I glared at him in mock annoyance and then explained about James coming to my rescue. When I finished my story, Grandpa smiled.

"Well, I am proud of both of my grandchildren who were involved in the talent show," he said.

I beamed, and James smiled sheepishly. Praise from Grandpa was its own reward. We ate quietly for a few minutes. Then I broke the silence.

"I've decided I enjoy singing for a group. I'd like to do it more often."

Grandpa pondered this for a moment before saying, "They're always looking for people to sing the special music at church."

"And at some youth events," James added.

"Great idea."

After thinking about it for the rest of the evening, I decided I would tell Lee, our music/youth minister who insisted we call him by his first name, that I wanted to do just that. Lying in bed that night, I couldn't help but smile. I was pretty sure I had finally found *my thing*, and it felt just as good as I'd always imagined.

4

—A WEEKEND TO REMEMBER

The following Sunday, I went to church with one mission: talk to Lee about opportunities to sing. Unfortunately, my cousins and I walked in the church gym just as Sunday school was starting. As I hurried to find a seat, I knew I'd probably have to wait until Sunday school and the church service were over before I could talk to Lee. I shot a glare at the back of Billy's blond head. If he'd gotten up sooner, we could have arrived early, like I wanted. Pushing aside my disappointment, I focused on what Lee was saying.

"Last, I'm excited to announce that we'll be having a Disciple Youth weekend in February. I'll share more details in a few weeks, but go ahead and tell your parents about it now."

I smiled, making a mental note to tell Grandpa about the upcoming event after church. I'd attended every Disciple Youth event since I joined the youth group in sixth grade, but this year would be different. This year, I would get to be a part of the high school group for the first time.

"Now," Lee continued. "I'd like everyone to turn to Acts chapter twelve."

Taking out my Bible, I did my best to pay attention

to the Sunday school lesson. When it was over, I walked toward the front podium as fast as I could, but as usual, Lee made a beeline for the sanctuary, barely speaking to anyone. Resigned to wait, I went to join Grandpa and my cousins in our customary pew.

When the service was finally over, I made sure to go out the door where Lee was shaking hands instead of the main door that was Pastor Benjamin's domain. I had to wait for several people to shake Lee's hand on their way out. By the time it was my turn, I was trembling with nerves. I wanted opportunities to sing so badly, and this was my best chance.

"Good to see you today, Ally," Lee said as the elderly man in front of me slowly made his way toward the parking lot.

"Thanks." I paused in the doorway.

"Something on your mind?" Lee asked, a knowing look in his eyes.

"Well," I said, fidgeting with my skirt pocket, "I...uhhh...wanted to tell you that—that if you ever need anyone to sing special music or something, I—I'd like to."

"That's great, Ally." Lee smiled. "I'll be sure to add you to my list." He thought for a second. "As a matter of fact, why don't you go ahead and plan to sing the special music on Youth Sunday at the end of Disciple Youth weekend?"

I beamed at him. This was better than I could have hoped for.

"OK. Thank you, Lee." I started to leave but then turned back to look at him. "What song should I sing?"

Miriam Thor

"That's up to you. Pray about it, and let me know once you decide so I can get the background track for you."

"Sounds great. Thanks!" I walked to the car, grinning like a madwoman.

"What are you so happy about?" Billy asked as I climbed into the backseat. The entire family had apparently been waiting on me.

"Lee said I can sing the special music on Youth Sunday."

Billy stared at me, clearly at a loss as to why I found that so exciting. Fortunately for him, Grandpa spared him the necessity of responding.

"That's great." Grandpa pulled out of the parking space. "I look forward to hearing you sing this time."

"Thanks," I told him, already debating which song I should choose for my church debut.

By the time I went to bed that night, I'd already chosen a song, one I already knew by heart. I told Lee which song I chose Wednesday night at youth group, and he had the CD for me by the following Sunday. All that was left for me to do was to practice my heart out. And I did. Not quite as much as I did for the talent show but enough that I could definitely sing the song in my sleep by the time Disciple Youth weekend arrived.

That Friday evening, Billy drove us to the church in his car, an old sports car he'd spent his life savings on a few weeks earlier. It was a bucket of bolts that might at one time have been blue but was now a combination of gray and rust. Billy thought it was the best car in the world and was eager to show it off to his friends once we arrived at church. I thought we were lucky to make it there without breaking down and decided I would ride home from church with Grandpa on Sunday.

As soon as my cousins and I walked into the church gym, Billy went to join his friends, which I was glad to see included Austin Peterson. In my opinion, Austin was the epitome of tall, dark, and handsome. I couldn't help having a crush on him, even though Billy wouldn't let anything come of it.

Watching Billy with his friends, I felt a twinge of jealousy. Whether we were at school or church, Billy always had people to hang out with. I wasn't so fortunate. At school, I had Missy, of course, and a few other girls who welcomed me in their group, even if we weren't that close. At church, though, I often felt as if I didn't have a place to belong. The only other girls in my grade were Macie and Gracie, twin sisters who seemed to prefer each other's company over anyone else's. The girls in other grades were nice enough, but they all had their cliques from school that I wasn't a part of. And of course, Billy made sure that most of the boys gave me a wide berth.

"Come on," James said, still standing beside me by the door.

With a grateful nod, I followed him over to stand with Collin and Hunter, his two best friends. Unfortunately for James, they both attended a private school instead of going to Mayville High with us. Collin and Hunter were the only boys besides my cousins who weren't scared to look at me. James had assured Billy that neither of them harbored any romantic interest in me, and Billy had taken his word for it. They were both nice guys, a lot like James. Not the type to ask girls out unless they were sincerely interested in them. I figured that was the real reason Billy didn't mind me hanging out with them. That and the fact that James was always there to play chaperone.

"Hey," Collin said as we walked up.

"Hey," James said. "Do you know — ?"

"Welcome to Disciple Youth," Lee shouted over the din. "Before we do anything else tonight, we're having pizza." He pointed at a table at the back of the gym where a lot of pizza boxes were stacked. "So, I'll pray, and then you can have at it."

Lee said a quick blessing, and we all raced for the table. The pizza was good, and the worship time afterward was even better. Instead of our usual praise band, a group of college students led the music, and one of them spoke afterward. It was cool hearing from someone so close to my age who wasn't on staff at a church.

When worship was over, Lee divided us into groups based on gender and whether we were in middle or high school. Each group was assigned to a different college student leader and adult chaperone. With trepidation, I said good-bye to James and his friends and went to stand with the high school girls' group.

"Hi," our leader said as soon as we were all assembled. "I'm Erin, and I'm looking forward to getting to know all of you this weekend."

"And as I'm sure you all know, I'm Mrs. Annie," our chaperone chimed in. "And you'll be staying at my house for the weekend."

I glanced at Lily, Mrs. Annie's eleventh-grade daughter, to see what she thought of this arrangement. To my surprise, she didn't seem to mind having her mom watching us all weekend.

"We're going to have a lot of fun this weekend," Erin said. "And, hopefully, you'll learn a lot about Jesus and maybe a little about yourselves, too. Now let's go."

She led us out to the parking lot, and the ten girls in our group were divided between Mrs. Annie's van and her husband's truck. Erin followed us to their house in her car. We played a few get-to-know-you games and had a short devotion before bed. As I tucked myself into my sleeping bag, I decided this weekend might be a good chance for me to get to know the other girls in my youth group better. My last thought before I fell asleep was that I couldn't wait until Sunday so I could sing for the whole church.

The next morning, the entire youth group met back at the church for a quick morning worship session. Then we divided back into our groups for a scavenger hunt that took us all over Mayville and had us do crazy things like order one French fry at a fast-food restaurant and get five dollars' worth of pennies from a bank. I earned my group's respect by agreeing to jump into a swimming pool. Since it was February, the water was freezing, but the smiles on their faces as

I got out and dried myself off were totally worth it.

When the scavenger hunt was over, all the groups met at the park. As we ate hot dogs, Lee announced that the winner of the scavenger hunt was the high school boys' group but that the high school girls were a close second. He then told us we were free to do whatever we chose for the next few hours at the park as long as we were careful.

Feeling content, I threw away my trash and walked over to where James was sitting with his friends.

"Congratulations," I told them.

"On?" James asked.

"Winning the scavenger hunt." I wondered where he'd been all morning.

"Right. Thanks. But you should probably congratulate Billy more than me. He led the team to victory. I just went along for the ride."

"We all did," Hunter said, taking a swig of soda.

"That's really all you can do with Billy and Austin at the helm," Collin added. "Well, with one exception. I still can't believe you refused to jump in the pool, James."

I frowned, tension coiling in my stomach. "Only one person had to jump in the pool. Why would it matter if it was James?"

"Austin wanted all of us to jump in," Hunter explained. "He said the judges might give us bonus points for it."

"But James shot that idea down real quick," Collin said. "Austin looked ready to explode until Billy helped him cool off...literally."

I raised my eyebrows.

"He pushed him in the pool," James said. "Our leader took a picture of it, and we left for our next stop." He shrugged as if it wasn't a big deal.

I studied my cousin. He could pretend all he wanted, but we both knew the situation had been more serious than either of his friends knew. Before he came to live with Grandpa, James had witnessed his dad and little sister drown, and he hadn't put a toe in water deeper than a bathtub ever since. I met his gaze, silently asking if he was OK. He gave a tiny nod of affirmation and changed the subject.

"So, what do you want to do this afternoon?"

"I'm not sure," I said, letting myself relax. "I think I'll see what the other girls are planning."

"Are you interested in going out in a paddle boat?" Hunter asked, looking at me.

I stared at him, stunned. The two of us alone in a boat? Despite James's assurance, Billy would probably kill him. Hunter must have read my thoughts on my face because he quickly shook his head.

"Not you and me," he clarified. "It would be you and James. I was hoping to go out on the water, but there's only two people per boat. So, I thought—"

"I'm not really in the mood to paddle boat," James interrupted.

If I didn't know him so well, his voice would have sounded nonchalant.

"But you two should go," he told his friends. "And Ally, it looks as though the other girls are playing volleyball." He nodded his head toward the net where the other high school girls were choosing teams.

"You sure?" Collin asked, his gaze on James.

"Yeah," he said. "I didn't sleep that well last night, so I'm taking it easy."

"All right." Collin and Hunter headed toward the pier.

I gazed at my cousin in concern.

"I'm good, Ally," he insisted. "Now go kick butt in volleyball."

"OK."

The subject was closed. With a small sigh, I jogged over to the net.

At the end of our first game, I glanced over.

James had settled with his back against a tree without a book or any other form of entertainment. Knowing James, he was probably listening to the wind or something.

Shaking my head, I focused on the second game.

Midway through our third game, I heard a commotion and looked around for the source. What I saw had me sprinting toward the lake before I made a conscious decision to move. Austin had James's arms pinned behind his back and was forcing him toward the lake, obviously planning to throw him in. James was struggling, but Austin was a year older and a lot bigger than he was. A few other boys were standing around, laughing as they watched the scene unfold.

"Let him go," I yelled.

Since my cries had no effect, I closed the remaining distance and latched onto Austin's arm.

"Let him go," I repeated, tugging at arms that seemed to be made of granite.

Austin shook me off. "He didn't want to go in the pool this morning, so he can go in the lake instead," he said, earning snickers from the onlookers.

Panic raced down my spine. James couldn't swim, and he might very well freeze in terror once he was in the water. He could die from this stupid prank. I looked around for a stick or rock, anything I could use as a weapon, and saw Billy barreling toward us. I had never been so happy to see my oldest cousin in my life.

Billy wrenched Austin away from James and shoved him hard enough to send him staggering back a few paces. Then he set himself between the two, his narrowed eyes daring Austin to try to get past him.

"What's the matter with you, Billy?" Austin demanded. "I was just going to throw him in the water. It's not as though I planned to drown him."

I looked at James. He was already pale and shaking. Hearing Austin's words, what little color he had left drained from his face.

Billy clenched his fists. "I don't care what you planned to do." His voice was low and dangerous. "What matters to me is that James didn't want to do it, and you were forcing him to."

"It's not a big deal," Austin said, crossing his arms. "Let it go."

Billy glanced back at James, a question in his eyes. I recognized the look. It was the same one Billy had given me the day he'd caught Myron Wilcox picking on me. The one that said he would gladly teach the one who had hurt his family a lesson with his fists, but only if we wanted him to.

When Billy had given me that look, I'd nodded instantly, wanting Myron to pay in blood for making me cry.

James just shook his head. *No,* he seemed to say. *It's not worth it.*

Billy unclenched his fists and looked back at Austin. "All right, I'll let it go this time." The glare he threw at Austin and the onlookers said there better not be a next time.

Austin bristled but walked away, his cronies on his heels.

Billy and I both turned to look at James, who was doing his best to look OK when we knew he wasn't.

"You want to go home?" Billy asked him, his eyes filled with concern.

James took a shaky breath and shook his head.

"You sure?" Billy asked, looking him up and down.

James took a couple more breaths and then met his gaze. "I'm sure."

"All right," Billy said. "Let me know if you change your mind or if Austin or any of the others mess with you again."

James shook his head. "I can fight my own battles, Billy. Although I *do* appreciate your help today. The water..." His gaze flicked toward the lake, and he shuddered.

Billy gripped James's upper arm. "I know. Don't worry about it."

James nodded. "I need to sit down," he said and walked off.

When he was out of earshot, Billy looked at me. "Next time, come get me."

"But—"

"Most guys won't stop just because you say so," he said. "Especially Austin. I mean it, Ally. Come get me."

"There probably won't be a next time," I told him. "I don't think Austin meant any harm. He doesn't know about James's phobia."

Although he had seemed to enjoy James's panic a little too much. My crush on him evaporated. I had no interest in dating a guy who took pleasure in tormenting others.

"That's true, but if there is—"

"I'll come get you." I gave in. I had to admit my protests hadn't been effective.

"Good," he said. "Now, why don't you go back to your volleyball game? From what I saw, you were doing pretty well."

"Thanks." I flashed him a grin. "I'm surprised you were able to pull your attention away from Lily and Rachel long enough to notice."

He snorted. "A guy has to figure out who to ask to prom somehow."

"Good luck with that," I told him, and we went our separate ways.

Not long after that, each group returned to their host family's house to eat a quick dinner and clean up.

Then we went back to the church for another

worship session.

As the band played the first song, I studied James out of the corner of my eye. He was singing with his eyes closed. He'd told us it helped him focus on God. Relieved that he seemed to be back to normal, I started singing myself.

The rest of the worship session and our devotion that night passed quickly for me. Before I knew it, I was lying in my sleeping bag and trying to calm my nerves enough to sleep. *Lord,* I prayed, *please help everything go well when I sing tomorrow.*

With my song playing in my head, I drifted off to sleep.

We didn't have normal Sunday school the next morning. Instead, we spent the time preparing for the upcoming student-led worship service. The praise band set up their equipment and had a quick rehearsal. I practiced my song once, and the students who'd agreed to share their testimonies said the first sentence or two into the microphone to make sure they were used to the way it sounded. By the time we finished all that, people were filing into the sanctuary for the service, and I was trembling with a combination of nerves and anticipation.

Since I would be performing during the service, I sat with James and the rest of the praise band on the second row instead of joining the rest of the youth group a few rows back.

"Calm down, Ally," James said, putting a hand on my shoulder. "You'll do fine."

"I hope so." I bit my lip to help my nerves.

If everything went well today, it would confirm that singing for an audience was my thing. With all my heart, I wanted things to go without a hitch.

"You will," James assured me as Lee walked up to the podium to begin the service.

I gave him a small smile to express my gratitude. Sometimes, I wasn't sure what I would do without James's support.

After Lee welcomed everyone to Youth Sunday, he called the praise band up to lead the congregation in worship. I sang along, but my mind was on my upcoming performance. More than once, I stopped singing and prayed that my song would go well.

When the praise band finished their last song, Hunter went to the podium to say a prayer. While everyone's eyes were closed, the praise band left the stage, and I walked onto it, just as we rehearsed. I picked up the microphone and waited, my heart beating wildly.

The intro music for my song started as soon as Hunter said amen. I surveyed the congregation in front of me. It was smaller than the crowd at the talent show but not by much. Grandpa was in our usual pew, looking expectant, while almost everyone else just looked politely interested.

Then I caught James's eye. He smiled and gave me an encouraging nod. He knew I could do this, and suddenly, I did, too. When the music got to my cue, I opened my mouth and sang my heart out.

At the end of the song, everyone applauded. I made my way back to the second row and sat next to

James.

I had finally found my thing.

Thank You, Lord, I prayed and smiled in contentment.

My first year of high school had been a huge success so far, and everything was right in my little world.

~March 31, 2019; 7:15 a.m.~

Bang. The door to the hall closes, jolting me from my reverie. It's dark in Grandpa's hospital room, but with the pale morning light from the window, I see a broad-shouldered outline with wavy blond hair. Billy.

I sigh with relief and move toward him. As he wraps me in a tight bear hug, I notice that he's wearing his fireman uniform. His shirt is wet because of the rain outside, but I don't care. I'm just grateful he's here.

"How is he?" he asks.

"The doctors say the first twenty-four hours are critical. If he can make it that long, they'll have hope."

He steps back and looks down at me. "I'm sorry you've had to deal with this on your own, Ally. It—"

I cut him off. "You couldn't have gotten here any faster. You live three hours away, and you clearly had to work last night. I'm fine."

He nods, reluctant to admit the truth of my words, and then walks toward the bed to look down at Grandpa.

"It's so weird seeing him like this," he mutters. "Grandpa's always been so strong. I just didn't think something like this could happen to him."

A tear rolls down my cheek. "Pray with me, Billy," I beg as I look down to hide my wet eyes. "I've been praying, but I've always felt that our prayers are more powerful as a family."

He walks back to the foot of the bed to stand next to me, and we turn to face each other. Grandpa's to my left and his right, just like always, but the circle is incomplete. We both gaze at that empty space and back at each other. As I meet Billy's eyes, I know he's remembering the same thing I am. Without a word, he shakes his head as if to clear it, walks over beside the bed, and sits down in another of those not-so-comfortable chairs. I return to mine, and we sit in silence, remembering the other time there was an empty space in the circle.

5

—THE LONGEST WEEK OF MY LIFE

~May 2, 2015~

In what seemed like no time, we only had three weeks of school left before summer break. On the first Saturday in May, Grandpa decided we needed to get all the necessary chores done, so we would have plenty of free time during the following weeks to study for finals. For some reason, he seemed to think that more free time would lead to more studying. While I doubted that was the case, I knew better than to argue.

That morning, Billy pulled weeds in the garden while James repaired several holes in the roof of the barn. I did a variety of things including washing dishes, cleaning the bathroom, and doing laundry. Grandpa "supervised" from the front porch, which he said was a privilege of old age.

At noon, we all took a break for lunch. As we sat around the table eating sandwiches, I could tell Billy and James were extremely glad to be in the air-conditioned indoors. On closer inspection, James looked exhausted, as if he might fall asleep mid-swallow.

"You OK?" I asked him.

He didn't respond.

"James...James!" I repeated.

He jumped a little. "What?"

"Are you OK?"

"Yeah, I'm fine," he said. "Just a headache. It's hot out there."

I looked at Billy and Grandpa to see if they believed him, but they were engrossed in their sandwiches.

"Maybe you should stay inside for a while and wash dishes or something after lunch," I suggested.

He shook his head. "No, I need to get all the holes in the barn roof patched. It's supposed to rain tomorrow."

We lapsed into silence. When we finished eating, we all went back to our chores. I didn't think any more about James. I figured he knew what he was doing. Besides, it was hard to think about anything while cleaning out a refrigerator full of old, and sometimes moldy, food. I had just thrown away a container of peas that had mysterious white fuzz on them when Grandpa asked me to go sweep out the barn. Gratefully, I shut the refrigerator and went to do so.

As I walked outside, I looked for my cousins. Billy was weeding the last row of vegetables in the garden. I smiled, thinking that maybe when he was finished, he'd clean out the rest of the refrigerator for me.

James was at the very top of the barn roof, still patching holes. He stood up straight, wiped the sweat from his brow, and then swayed a little as if he was dizzy.

"James!" I yelled, concerned.

He didn't seem to hear me, but Billy did. He turned and looked in James's direction at the very moment James collapsed.

"James!" I shrieked, as he slid down the barn's slanted roof.

With speed and reflexes born from his many hours on the football field, Billy dashed to the ladder James had used to get on top of the barn. His feet barely touched the rungs as he scrambled to the roof just in time to keep James from sliding off. How he did it, I had no idea. Maybe God sent angels to carry him from the ladder to the roof because I had never seen him move that fast.

"James!" he yelled and shook his shoulders. "James, wake up!" No response.

"Is he OK? Is he OK?" I was nearly hysterical.

Billy answered in a voice that shook. "I don't know." He continued to shake him. "I don't think so. Go call 911!"

I rushed inside, picked up the phone, and dialed.

Grandpa was at the kitchen sink washing the lunch dishes. As soon as he saw me, he asked what was wrong.

I pointed out the window as a female on the phone said, "Nine-one-one emergency, how may I help you?"

Grandpa took off running faster than I'd ever seen.

"My cousin," I said, trying to force down my panic. "He passed out. We don't know what's wrong. He needs help. He—"

"OK, ma'am," the voice interrupted. "We'll send

help. Where do you live?"

I gave her the address and hung up. Then I ran back outside.

Billy and Grandpa were attempting to get James off the barn roof. Billy had his hands beneath James's armpits while Grandpa held his feet. Slowly, they lowered him off the edge, brought him down the ladder, and set him gently on the ground.

I stood beside them the whole time, trying to steady the ladder and be ready to catch them if they fell, although I had no clear idea how I'd do that.

By the time the ambulance arrived, they'd gotten James to the ground.

"What happened?" one of the paramedics asked, kneeling next to James.

"He passed out," I said through numb lips. "He was working on the roof of the barn, and—"

"Did he fall off the barn?" Another paramedic ran his hands along the back of James's neck.

"No," Billy said. "He was at the top of the roof when he collapsed. He slid down pretty far, but I stopped him before he went over the edge."

The paramedic nodded. "Good, it should be safe to move him. Anything else?"

"He worked outside all morning, and he seemed out of it at lunch," I said, not sure if it was relevant.

The guy nodded again. "Let's get him on the board," he told one of his coworkers.

They moved James onto the stretcher and headed for the ambulance.

"What's his name?" a female paramedic asked as

they loaded him on.

"James Griffin," Grandpa said.

She nodded. "You can meet us at the hospital." She slammed the doors.

I suppressed a sob as the ambulance drove away.

"This is my fault," I said despairingly. "I knew something wasn't right at lunch. I should've—"

"It's not your fault, Ally," Grandpa said, putting a hand on my shoulder.

Billy seemed too shocked to say anything.

I'm not really sure how we got to the hospital. Grandpa drove and Billy rode shotgun. I sat alone in the backseat, crying silently. All I could see was James swaying and falling over and over again. My own horrific version of instant replay. *Please, God,* I prayed silently. *Please let him be OK. Please. Please.*

When we arrived at the hospital, the nurse at the desk in the emergency room told us that the doctor was with James and that he would come talk to us as soon as he knew anything.

Grandpa thanked her, and then we all sat together in the waiting room.

I glanced around at the tile floors and white walls, trying to make myself believe this was actually happening.

Several other people were sitting in chairs around the room, including a couple with a squalling toddler. There was a TV hanging in one corner of the room, but I couldn't bring myself to care what was on. All I could do was pray.

Please, God. Please. Please.

A tall gray-haired doctor came to talk to us after about fifteen minutes. He said that James was severely dehydrated and had suffered from heat exhaustion.

"That means you can give him some fluids, and he'll be OK, right?" Grandpa asked.

Hope stirred in my chest. Grandpa had served in the Marines and spent a lot of time outside over the course of his life. Surely, he knew what he was talking about.

The doctor sighed. "I wish it were that simple."

My heart sank.

"We found a contusion on James's head. It would seem he hit his head when he fell. We've tried to wake him up without success," the doctor continued. "I'm worried that he could have a concussion or swelling in the brain. We'll have to run some tests to know exactly what's going on."

I clenched my teeth to keep from screaming.

"Can we see him?" Grandpa asked.

The doctor shook his head. "I'm sorry. We need to start the tests right away. I'll let you know as soon as we know something." He walked away.

I tried to process what he'd told us. My brain just couldn't seem to accept that this was really happening. The three of us sat in the waiting room without speaking. People came and went. Doctors and nurses rushed by us, intent on their jobs. Hour after hour passed, and still we heard nothing.

Please, God. Please, please.

At long last, the doctor came out and walked over. "We did a CT scan and an MRI," he said. "James has some swelling in his brain. He woke up during the tests, but because of the swelling, we've sedated him. We'd like to keep him sedated while giving him fluids and medication to reduce the swelling."

We all stared at him, too stunned to respond.

"We'll have to monitor him closely, so he'll need to stay in the ICU."

Grandpa managed to nod. "Can we see him?"

"Yes, one at a time and only for a minute," the doctor said.

Grandpa nodded again.

"Will he be OK?" Billy asked, speaking for the first time since the ambulance left our house.

The doctor frowned. "It's too soon to tell. The swelling isn't too severe, and James is young and strong, which will work in his favor. The swelling should go down over the next few days, but with brain injuries, it's impossible to be sure. I wish I could give you a definitive answer, but I honestly don't know."

Billy stood up, his fists clenched. "You don't know? It's your job to know, you…" He said words students at school only said with no teacher around.

"William Timothy!" Grandpa said in a steely voice.

Billy sat down hard and ran a hand through his hair.

"I'm sorry," Grandpa said.

The doctor shook his head. "I understand." He looked at Billy. "I promise we'll do everything we can for him." He turned to Grandpa. "I'll take you to see him now."

Wordlessly, we followed him. He led us to an elevator, and we took it to the third floor, the Intensive Care Unit.

When the doors opened, the doctor turned right and walked down the hall with us trailing behind him. He stopped outside of room 312. "This is James's room," he said, opening the door. "Who's going in first?"

"I am," Grandpa said and went in before I even had the chance to process the question. The doctor went in too and shut the door behind him.

I looked at Billy, unsure what to do.

"You go next." His jaw was clenched so tight that he could barely get the words out.

I nodded. I should have tried to persuade him to go before me, but I couldn't. I just had to see James.

Grandpa came out after about a minute. His face was ashen as he held the door open for me.

I took a deep breath and forced my legs to move. I stopped at the foot of the bed. As much as I'd wanted to see James, I couldn't bear to look at my cousin right away. I glanced around the room, trying to find something else to focus on. The room was dimly lit. There was a framed painting on the wall that showed a mare and her foal grazing in front of a barn. I'm sure it was supposed to be soothing, but all it did for me was bring back the image of James falling.

Taking a deep breath, I forced my gaze away from the painting and onto my cousin. James was lying on his back with several wires and tubes connected to him. I did my best to ignore those and look at his face.

He had a scrape on his right cheek where it had raked against the shingles, and he was deathly pale. Otherwise, he looked normal.

I knew I should say something, but try as I might, I could think of nothing.

After what might have been an eternity or a minute, the doctor gently touched my shoulder. "It's time to go," he said.

Fighting back tears, I walked back to the hall, pausing to hold the door for Billy on my way out. I breathed hard, trying not to sob.

Grandpa put his arm around my shoulders, and I lost the battle and let the tears come. We stayed like that until Billy and the doctor came out a minute later. Billy's fists were clenched as tight as his jaw.

The doctor looked at us kindly.

"It's getting late. You should go home and try to sleep. Come back in the morning. Hopefully, we'll know more by then."

Grandpa frowned. "But—"

"James isn't in any immediate danger," the doctor said. "His condition is unlikely to change overnight, but if something does happen, we'll call you."

Grandpa still looked unconvinced.

I didn't really want to leave either, but I knew staying in a waiting room all night would be hard on Grandpa's aging body. "Let's go home, Grandpa," I said, tugging lightly on his arm.

He sighed, but nodded and headed for the car.

It was well past dinner time when we got home. We weren't hungry, but we forced ourselves to eat a little anyway. None of us knew what to do with ourselves after that. We finally settled on watching TV, but I doubt any of us even knew what show was on. If the hottest guy in the world had walked across the screen, I wouldn't have noticed.

Around nine, Grandpa turned off the TV and suggested we pray together. We knelt on the rug in a triangle. Grandpa tried to pray, but his voice caught in his throat. We all stared at the spot James usually filled.

"Father," Grandpa whispered after a minute, "our prayers are too desperate for words tonight. Please hear our hearts instead."

We sat in silence then. Tears coursed down my cheeks as I repeated my prayer over and over again.

Please, God. Let him be OK. Please. Please.

After maybe ten minutes, Grandpa got up and walked to his room.

Billy and I looked at each other. More than anything, I wanted him to hug me and tell me it would be all right, but I knew he wouldn't. This was Billy, not James. Silently, I went to my room and crawled into bed. Despite how exhausted I was, I lay awake for hours thinking and praying. I didn't think I would ever fall asleep, but I guess I did.

When I woke up the next morning, it took me a second to figure out why I felt so worried. Then, it all came back to me in a rush. James falling, our time in the emergency room, how James had looked in the ICU. With a sigh, I got up and walked to the living room where I found Billy, sitting on the couch with dark circles under his eyes.

"Did you sleep at all?" I asked him.

He shook his head sharply.

"That's not good, Billy. You—"

"I'm fine, Ally!" he snapped. "I am fine." He closed his eyes, a pained expression on his face. I sat down next to him, unsure what else to do.

Please, God. Please. Please.

Grandpa got up not long after that. He fixed each of us some scrambled eggs, which we picked at and then threw away. Once breakfast was over, we all got ready and piled into the car to go to the hospital. Billy drove this time.

When we got there, we took the elevator to the third floor. Instead of going straight to James's room, Grandpa walked to the nurses' station near the elevator. "We're here to see James Griffin."

She checked her clipboard. "Are you his family?"

I nodded as Grandpa said, "Yes."

She smiled at us kindly. "Wait here a moment. I'll call Dr. Blakely."

I swallowed hard.

Please, God. Please. Please.

A different doctor than the one from the previous day walked up to us.

"Mr. Griffin," he said, looking at Grandpa. "I'm Dr. Blakely. I'll be James's doctor for the rest of his time here. I'd like to talk to you alone for a minute, please." He glanced at Billy and me, clearly expecting us to leave.

My whole body tensed. What could be so bad that

he didn't want us to know about it?

Billy glared at him. "We're not going anywhere. James is our family, too."

I nodded firmly in agreement.

"Billy," Grandpa said wearily. "Please just—"

"No." Billy's eyes were as hard as flint.

"Son," Dr. Blakely said, "walk down the hall with your sister for a minute. Your grandfather and I need to talk."

"I'm not your son," Billy said. "And we're staying."

Despite the gravity of the situation, I was touched that he didn't correct the man's assumption that I was his sister.

Dr. Blakely took a deep breath. "The adults need to talk. Now take a walk on your own, or I'll help you."

Billy raked his gaze over Dr. Blakely, sizing him up. He was a thin middle-aged man with a receding hairline. "Good luck with that," Billy said without budging.

"Never mind," Grandpa said. "They're old enough to hear this. How's James?"

Dr. Blakely frowned, unhappy at being overruled. "James has cerebral edema, which is also known as swelling in his brain. Because of that, we have him sedated and are giving him medication to reduce the swelling."

I gritted my teeth. We knew that already.

"Luckily, his skull hasn't sustained any fractures, so we hope the swelling will go down on its own over the next week," Dr. Blakely added. "Then we'll be able to assess the damage."

I bit the inside of my cheek until it bled. Damage? Brain damage?

Grandpa seemed to be thinking the same thing. "What kind of damage could there be?" he asked, his voice husky.

"It's not wise to speculate," Dr. Blakely said. "We'll know more when the swelling goes down, but we won't know for sure until we wake him up."

A buzzing sound filled my ears. "When do you think that'll be?" I heard myself ask.

Dr. Blakely shook his head. "I honestly don't know. It depends on how quickly the swelling goes down."

Billy glared at him, but he didn't yell profanity, so overall, I thought he handled it better than the last I-don't-know.

"Can we see him?" Grandpa asked.

"You can go in for a few minutes," Dr. Blakely said. "Follow me." He led us down the hall to room 312 and opened the door.

Grandpa and Billy went in without hesitating, so I took a deep breath and followed them. The room looked exactly as it had the night before. James did, too, except with it being brighter in the room, I could see a dark bruise behind his right ear. I stared at my cousin's face, willing him to open his eyes.

Please, God. Please. Please.

Suddenly, I couldn't take it anymore. It wasn't natural for him to be like this. It wasn't right. With tears in my eyes, I turned, ran out of the room, and didn't stop running until I was standing outside our car. Then I leaned against the right rear door and tried to get hold of myself. By the time Billy and Grandpa joined me, I had stopped crying, although I was still breathing hard.

Billy unlocked the car without a word, and we all got in.

"Dr. Blakely said there's no reason for us to stay," Grandpa told me as we drove out of the parking lot. "James is stable, and they'll call us if anything happens. Since we're still not allowed to stay in the room with him, I figured we might as well go home."

I nodded, not trusting myself to speak.

"Is that really hospital policy?" Billy asked. "Or just Dr. Blakely's? Honestly, that man has as much compassion as Hitler. I want the doctor I insulted last night back."

I glanced at Grandpa, expecting him to reprimand Billy, but he just sighed. Apparently, he didn't like Dr. Blakely any more than the rest of us.

For the remainder of the trip home, Billy drove silently.

I managed not to cry the whole time, but it was a near thing. As soon as we pulled in the driveway, Billy made a beeline for the barn while Grandpa and I headed for the house. When we got inside, Grandpa went to his room, saying that he wanted to lie down.

I just stood there in the kitchen, not knowing what to do. Finally, I decided to go out to the barn, hoping Billy was working on some chores I could help with.

As I neared the barn, I heard banging. Alarmed, I

ran to the doorway and froze.

Billy stood on the opposite side of the barn, facing the rear wall. He was punching the boards again and again, regardless of the damage he was causing to both the barn and his hands.

"Billy," I yelled. "Stop it!" He ignored me, so I ran over to him. "Stop it! Stop it!" I shrieked, trying to grab his arm and physically prevent him from continuing. Slowly, he stopped punching the wall and looked at me.

"Why?" he asked through clenched teeth.

"Because you're bleeding and—"

"No!" he interrupted. "Why? Why is James hurt? Why is God letting this happen?"

I shook my head, fresh tears starting down my cheeks. "I don't know," I whispered.

Billy sank to his knees. "Why?" he repeated. His questions seemed to be directed more to God than me. "Why?" And then he broke down in tears.

This shocked me more than anything. Billy never cried. Ever. I put my arms around him and cried, too. I wanted to say something to comfort him, to assure him that James would be all right, that God was in control. But the words died in my throat.

James who had always been there for me, who always knew when something was wrong. The question formed in my mind, too. *Why God? Why did You let him get hurt like this?*

I heard no answer. Looking down, I noticed blood in the hay. With a tremendous effort, I let go of Billy. "Let's go in the *–sniff–* house, so I can wrap-*sniff-* your hands."

He shook his head. "They're fine."

The sound of a throat clearing behind us startled me. We both turned toward the door. There stood Grandpa holding a rag, a tube of ointment, and a roll of bandages.

"I figured we'd be needing these," he said with a sigh. He walked over to Billy and began wiping the blood away with the rag. "You probably don't remember, but you did this when you first moved here right after your parents died, too." He glanced at the barn wall. "Of course, you weren't so strong back then, so the wall of the barn looked a lot better than it does now." He gently put ointment on Billy's hands and wrapped them in bandages.

"Why, Grandpa?" Billy asked, his voice a whisper. "Why did God let James get hurt?"

Grandpa shook his head, tears glistening in his eyes. "I don't know. The Almighty has never seen fit to tell me exactly why things happen, but I know He's here for us now, no matter what else happens."

I sighed deeply, hearing the truth in his words.

Please, God. Please. Please.

Grandpa frowned at Billy's hands. "I don't know how you'll hold a pencil at school tomorrow."

"School?" Billy repeated incredulously.

Grandpa nodded.

"We can't go to school tomorrow," I protested. "What about James?"

Grandpa frowned. "We can only visit James for a few minutes at a time. There will be plenty of time for that after you get home."

I stared at him, completely at a loss. How could we possibly go to school as though nothing had happened?

"You can't seriously expect us to go to school." Billy's face mirrored my disbelief. "We won't be able to pay attention enough to learn anything."

Grandpa heaved a sigh. "I understand how you feel, but hanging around here isn't doing either of you any good. Besides that, you've got finals coming up."

"No, Grandpa," I pleaded. "We should at least wait until James is awake."

A tear slipped down Grandpa's cheek. "Baby," he said gently, "we have no idea when the swelling will go down enough for them to wake up James. You two can't put your lives on hold until that happens. I'm sorry, but you're going to school tomorrow, and that's final."

My shoulders slumped. I nodded, trying to hold back yet another round of tears.

Billy looked as though he wanted to argue, but he gave a reluctant nod as well.

"Let's go back to the house," Grandpa suggested and headed that way.

Billy looked at me. "I have a bad feeling about this."

I nodded. I did, too.

On Monday morning when Grandpa woke us, I didn't remember about James for a few seconds. Then it came back to me, and I choked back tears and forced myself to get out of bed. I got ready mechanically, not caring what I wore or what my hair looked like. Then Billy and I walked to the bus stop without saying a word.

When I sat down next to Missy on the bus, she took one look at my face and asked what was wrong.

"James is in the hospital," I said, my lips quivering.

"What?" she asked, all the color draining from her face.

"He…he passed out on Saturday and hit his head. There's swelling in his brain, and they don't know when he'll wake up."

Missy took a deep breath. "We should pray." She took my hand and quietly prayed for God to heal James. Silently, I added my own plea.

Please, God. Please, please.

All day at school, I had to answer questions. My teachers wanted to know what was wrong. James's friends wanted to know where he was. Jenny wanted to know if I'd cried myself to sleep because she had a boyfriend and I didn't. By the end of the day, I was ready to write "James is in the hospital" on a poster and wear it around my neck. I would've done it too if I thought it would have helped.

When we got home from school, Grandpa took us to the hospital to see James. Dr. Blakely said that the swelling in James's brain had gone down a little and that the EEG—whatever that was—had picked up substantial brain activity. He also said that we could stay in James's room longer because he didn't need to be monitored as closely.

We stayed in his room for about an hour that day. Grandpa and I sat in the two comfortable-until-you-sit-in-them chairs while Billy leaned against a wall. We tried to talk to James just in case he could hear us. Mostly, we talked to each other, figuring that if James could hear, he would be interested whether we spoke directly to him or not. Whenever we reached a lull in the conversation, we'd all stare at James, wishing he would open his eyes.

Please, God. Please. Please.

When we went home, Billy and I did chores while Grandpa cooked supper. Billy did James's chores in addition to his own. When I tried to help, he barked at me that he could do them himself. Trying not to be offended, I decided that it helped him feel as if he was doing something useful and let him be. We spoke little during supper and then silently did our homework. When we finished, it was time for bed. We showered in our usual order—minus one—then prayed together, all too conscious of the empty space in the circle. As I crawled into bed that night, I kept praying.

Please, God. Please. Please.

The rest of the week followed pretty much the same pattern. The questions changed. People asked how James was doing instead of where he was or what was wrong. I tried and failed to pay attention all day, and then we went and saw James as soon as we got home. In every spare minute I had, I begged God to heal James, but as the week dragged on, I wasn't sure He heard me.

On Friday, I got called out of my fourth period

class to go to the office. As I walked up there, I tried desperately to remember if I'd done anything recently that would warrant being sent to the principal's office but couldn't think of a thing.

When I got to the office, Billy was sitting in a chair near the secretary's desk. He grinned as I walked in.

"James is awake."

I stared at him for a second as that simple statement sunk in, and then I smiled back at him as a tear rolled down my cheek. A happy tear.

"Mrs. MacDougall just told me," he said, inclining his head toward the secretary in case I didn't know who he was talking about. "Grandpa's coming to get us, so we can go to the hospital and see him."

As we waited together, I said another silent prayer.

Thank You, God. Thank You.

6

—THE SCARIEST THING HE NEVER HEARD

The moment that Grandpa walked into the office, I knew something was wrong. His face was stoic, and he was holding himself more rigidly than usual. I glanced at Billy in alarm. He shrugged one shoulder, his face showing the same confusion I felt.

After Grandpa signed us out, we followed him out of the building, waiting for him to say something. He didn't say a word as we crossed the parking lot. Once we got in the car and fastened our seatbelts, I couldn't wait any longer. "What's going on, Grandpa?" I asked.

He heaved a deep sigh as he backed out of the parking space.

"Mrs. MacDougall told me that James is awake," Billy said. "That's true, right?"

"He's awake," Grandpa's voice was carefully controlled.

Suddenly, I remembered Dr. Blakely's words about not being able to assess the damage until James woke up. "What's wrong with him, Grandpa?" I asked, trying to keep my voice steady.

"I don't know. Dr. Blakely says they'll have to run a lot of tests before they know exactly what areas of his brain have been affected."

"But he's OK, right?" Billy asked, his eyes practically burning a hole in Grandpa's head. "He's still…James, right?"

When Grandpa hesitated, I almost screamed. He had to still be James. The cousin I knew and loved and depended on. He had to be. "Grandpa!" I begged.

"Not exactly," Grandpa said, his voice soft. "In some ways, he seems the same, but sometimes the things he says just don't make a lick of sense." He blinked his eyes several times and cleared his throat.

I wanted to yell at him, to tell him that couldn't be true, but my throat seemed to have swelled shut.

"But it'll get better, right?" Billy asked. "With time, medicine, therapy, or…something. Right?" He was practically begging, too.

Grandpa glanced at us helplessly and then looked back at the road. "I don't know. Dr. Blakely said we would know more once they finished the tests, and in the meantime, we should try to behave as normally around James as possible. We have to act as if what he says makes sense even if it doesn't."

I forced myself to take a deep breath. "But how can we? If he's talking gibberish, how are we supposed to—?"

"The best we can," Grandpa said firmly. "Now try to get hold of yourselves. You need to act as normally as possible when you go in and see him. I know it'll be hard, so you don't have to stay very long."

We both nodded. I spent the rest of the ride praying for God to help me, help James, help all of us.

When we got to the hospital, Grandpa led the way to James's room and opened the door.

James was sitting up in bed with a lot less wires and tubes attached to him. The scrapes on his face had scabbed, and the bruise behind his ear had started to fade. He smiled when he saw us, but it seemed forced.

Despite everything Grandpa had said, I felt a surge of relief just seeing him conscious. "James." I rushed over to hug him.

He hugged me back but didn't say anything, which was odd. James always tried to comfort me when I was upset.

After several seconds, I pulled back. "It's so good to see you," I told him.

"I love you, too," he said.

I forced a smile.

"You gave us quite a scare," Billy said.

"Yeah," James said, sounding unsure, as though he didn't understand Billy's simple statement.

I glanced at Billy. His expression was neutral, but he had his fists clenched so tight that they trembled. James swallowed hard, and so did I. What did you say to someone who may or may not have brain damage?

"We went to school this week," Billy said when the silence became unbearable.

"School?" James repeated.

I nodded, grateful for the conversation starter.

"Yep," I babbled. "Everyone asked about you, and your teachers said not to worry. They'll work it out so you can be exempt from the work you missed and maybe even your finals. You'll still be able to go to eleventh grade next year."

Even as the words were coming out of my mouth, I knew it was the wrong thing to say. Who knew if James would even be able to go back to school next year?

"That's good," James said, but there was still a question in his voice.

Billy turned to look at me, his eyes saying "Shut up!" He tried to force his expression back to neutral before turning to look at James again. It didn't work.

James studied both of us and frowned, the way he always did when he knew something was wrong.

"Well," Grandpa said, trying to ease the tension, "Billy and Ally need to do their homework, so they'll be going home now. I'll just walk them downstairs." He looked at us meaningfully and strode toward the door.

"Bye, James," I said, waving at him and holding back tears.

"Bye," he said, still frowning.

"See ya," Billy started to follow me.

James was silent until we reached the door. "Billy, can I talk to you for a minute?" he said suddenly, as if he had to force the words out before he lost his nerve.

Billy froze. His expression looked a bit panicked, but he nodded. "Yeah, sure."

James looked at me expectantly.

Since his invitation didn't extend to me, I forced myself to walk out the door and close it, trying to hide my hurt and confusion. What could James need to tell Billy that he couldn't tell me? I glanced down the hall.

Grandpa was walking toward Dr. Blakely at the nurses' station, but there was no one else in sight. I hesitated for a second, knowing I should respect James's wish for privacy, but curiosity got the better of me. As quietly as possible, I eased the door open a crack and pressed my ear against it.

"What's up?" Billy asked.

Someone sighed, probably James.

"None of what I said made sense, did it?" he asked quietly.

Billy started pacing, his feet hitting the floor in measured steps. "Some of it did," he said after a second.

"Say that again but look right at me," James ordered.

I frowned. James never gave orders. And why would it matter if Billy looked at him?

Billy's footsteps stopped. "Some of it made sense," Billy repeated.

"Some of it?" James asked, seemingly for clarification, although Billy had already said it twice clear as day. Billy didn't say anything, but I assumed he nodded. James was quiet for a second. "They all think I'm crazy, don't they?" he asked.

"No," Billy said. "Not crazy...just...um..."

"I'm not crazy," James said, "Or whatever that stupid doctor thinks."

"No one said—"

James cut him off. "I can't hear," he said, a quiver in his voice.

"What?" Billy asked.

I stood paralyzed at the door, sure I'd misheard.

"I can't hear," James repeated. "I haven't heard anything since I woke up."

My stomach clenched.

"That's impossible," Billy said. "Hitting your head can't cause you to lose your hearing. Or if it did, it'll get better. You'll—"

"Billy," James said, his voice shaking even more. "I have no idea what you're saying. I have no idea what any of you have been saying. I tried to read your lips or guess what you might be saying, but that obviously didn't work. I don't know what I'll do—"

"James," Billy said. I heard the sound of flesh on flesh, as if Billy had tapped his arm. "Calm down. It'll be OK." He enunciated each word carefully. "We'll figure this out."

I wanted to run in there and hug James, to let him know that he wasn't alone, but I forced myself to remain where I was.

There was silence for a few seconds, and then Billy spoke again. "Why haven't you told the doctor?" he asked.

"What?" James sounded frustrated.

"The doctor," Billy repeated. I heard him moving around, presumably pantomiming the word.

"The doctor," James said.

"Why haven't you told him?" Billy said each word slowly.

James sighed. "Every time the doctor comes in here, he just talks and talks. He doesn't seem to care what I have to say. Grandpa's been here most of the morning, and I didn't want to upset him, and…and…"

"And what?" Billy asked.

"And saying it…telling them…makes it real." Another few seconds of silence seemed to go on forever.

"Do you want me to tell them?" Billy asked.

I'm not sure how James understood him, but he must have.

"You don't have to," James said. "I should just do it myself. I know it's a lot to ask."

I could almost hear Billy rolling his eyes. Only James could wake up unable to hear and still be worried about burdening someone else.

"I don't mind," Billy said. "I'll be back in a minute."

I heard footsteps coming toward the door and backed away just in time to avoid falling face forward into the room.

Billy looked at me suspiciously. "You heard?" he asked as he shut the door. When I nodded, he sighed. "Well, at least that's one less person I have to tell. Where's Grandpa?"

"Down there." I pointed toward the nurses' station.

Billy strode down the hall. After a brief internal debate, I followed him, unsure what else to do. Grandpa and Dr. Blakely were deep in discussion.

Billy walked straight up to them. "James can't hear," he said, interrupting their conversation. Billy never was one for beating around the bush.

"That's unlikely," Dr. Blakely said. "He has

symptoms of a processing or cognitive impairment. What makes you think he can't hear?"

"Well, for starters, he told me," Billy said.

"He did," I confirmed.

Dr. Blakely frowned. "He could be lying, trying to make excuses for the unusual things he's been saying."

James would never lie, especially about something this serious.

"Or he really can't hear," Billy said, annoyed, "so he didn't know what anyone was saying."

"He could be in denial," Dr. Blakely continued, ignoring Billy. "Trying to convince himself that he's not hearing what people say, and so that's the reason he doesn't understand them."

"I don't think James is the one in denial," Billy said.

Dr. Blakely sniffed disdainfully. "Look, boy, I have had years of experience with traumatic brain injuries. I really—"

"I don't care," Billy interrupted. "James wouldn't lie about this. Besides, he was completely coherent when we talked just now."

"He was?" Grandpa asked hopefully.

"Yeah," Billy said. "He had to ask me to repeat a few things, but otherwise he was fine."

"Asking you to repeat things can be a sign of an auditory processing problem," Dr. Blakely said.

Billy rolled his eyes. "Yeah. He can't hear anything, so his brain can't process it. That's the problem." He shook his head. "James is right. You don't care what he has to say. No wonder he didn't tell you."

If looks could kill, Billy would've dropped dead on the spot from the glare Dr. Blakely aimed at him. Since they couldn't, he didn't seem even slightly perturbed.

"We'll just go talk to James." Dr. Blakely stormed down the hall.

I decided that if the hospital gave an award to the person who insulted doctors most often, Billy was well on his way to winning it. I considered chastising him but decided against it. He wouldn't listen to me, and besides, I agreed with him.

Dr. Blakely entered James's room a few steps ahead of us and let the door shut in Grandpa's face. A very mature, adult way to handle the situation. Grandpa opened it without comment, and we all filed inside.

James was sitting up in bed, looking rather nervous.

Dr. Blakely stood at the foot of his bed. "Your brother tells me you *think* you can't hear," he said. "Is that true?" He made no effort to enunciate or slow down.

James glanced at Billy, his expression saying "You told him I can't hear, right?" Billy gave a slight nod, so James looked back at Dr. Blakely. "What?"

Dr. Blakely repeated what he'd said, again making no effort to help James understand his words.

James looked at us, confused by what was going on.

"He *knows* he can't hear," Billy told Dr. Blakely.

"Do you?"

Dr. Blakely rolled his eyes. "You said he was talking coherently with you as long as you repeated things. I repeated my question and looked right at him so he could read my lips. What's the problem?"

Billy rolled his eyes. "I spoke slower and used some gestures to help get my point across. You're not even trying—"

"So, what you're saying is that he can only understand you if you make extra effort to communicate," Dr. Blakely said. "That supports *my* theory of a cognitive or processing—"

"But if he can't hear," Grandpa chimed in, "that might explain why he—"

"My theories are *much* more likely," Dr. Blakely said. "His symptoms—"

Billy crossed his arms. "Would it really hurt your ego to admit we could be right about James being unable to hear?"

"Now, Billy," Grandpa chided, "you don't need to insult—"

"I know what I'm talking about," Dr. Blakely practically shouted, "and you need to..."

I lost track of the argument and glanced over at James. He was staring at all of them, his gaze darting back and forth in a vain attempt to follow the conversation. I imagined the situation from his perspective, sitting in silence watching the three of them yell at each other with no idea what was going on. Yeah, they were doing him a lot of good.

Scanning the room, I spotted a notepad sitting on

the rolling table next to the bed. I picked it up, found a pen in my purse, and wrote Dr. Blakely's question on it, exactly as he'd phrased it. When I was finished, I handed it to James.

He read it quickly and nodded. "Yeah, that's true."

I was the only one who heard him. The three males at the foot of the bed were too busy arguing to notice James had spoken at all. I wanted to throw a bucket of cold water on them to get their attention. It would've served them right, but since procuring a bucket would've taken too long, I decided to take a different approach. "All of you, shut up!" I yelled at the top of my lungs.

Everyone in the room froze and turned to stare at me.

"James would like to answer your question, Dr. Blakely." I nodded at James and pointed at the notepad.

"Yeah, that's true," James said. "I can't hear."

Dr. Blakely considered this. "What do you mean by that? Do people's words run together, so you can't understand them? Do words just not make sense?"

I snatched the notepad and started writing as soon as he spoke, but it took me several seconds to get it all down. When I finished, I showed it to James.

"No." James shook his head. "I can't hear you at all. It's as if I'm watching a TV on mute, except there's kind of a ringing sound."

Dr. Blakely's brows furrowed. "It's conceivable that a labyrinthine concussion could cause..." He continued talking for at least thirty seconds using terminology straight from a medical textbook.

James looked at me, confused, so I wrote "complicated medical stuff" on the notepad and showed it to him. He nodded his understanding.

Finally, Dr. Blakely remembered we were in the room. "We'll have to run several tests, but we should be able to verify that and give you more conclusive answers soon."

I summarized that into "need more tests" and held the notepad up for James to see. He nodded.

"I'll go schedule them," Dr. Blakely said and walked out.

We all looked at each other, unsure what to say until James broke the silence.

"Thanks, Ally," he said. When I looked puzzled, he pointed at the notepad. "I'm not sure we would've made any progress if you hadn't started writing down the questions."

"You're welcome," I said, glad that I could help him.

"I'm not sure I've ever heard you yell that loud," Billy told me.

I shrugged. "I needed your attention. You should just be glad there were no buckets of cold water available for me toss on you."

Billy and Grandpa chuckled, but James didn't respond. Of course, he didn't. He hadn't heard me.

"I'm sorry." I eyed him. "I didn't even think—"

"Don't worry about it, Ally. You can still talk to each other around me. It's fine."

It wasn't fine. I could see fear and frustration

carefully hidden behind his calm façade. He glanced at the clock. "Have you eaten lunch yet?"

We all shook our heads.

"You should go eat. And you don't have to come back right away. They'll just be running tests all afternoon." There was a hint of desperation behind his calm words, as if he knew he was telling us what he ought to but was terrified we might actually listen.

"We're not going anywhere," Grandpa told him.

I wrote that on the notepad and added some exclamation points. When James read it, his shoulders sagged in relief.

"He has a point about lunch, though," Billy said. "I could run and pick up some burgers or something."

Grandpa didn't normally splurge for fast food, but I guess he decided these were extenuating circumstances. He handed Billy the keys to his car and told him to hurry back.

I sat down in the chair on one side of James's bed, and Grandpa sat in the other. I picked up the notepad. "Are you in pain?" I wrote to James on the notepad.

He read it and shrugged. "My head hurts some," he admitted, "but they gave me some medicine, so it's not too bad."

I nodded, and we sat in awkward silence. At least I thought it was awkward. It was impossible to tell what the other two thought. James had always been the quietest of us, and Grandpa never made small talk. He said it was a waste of perfectly good air.

Billy came back a half hour later. He handed Grandpa and me our burgers. "The nurse at the desk said James couldn't have one. Someone will bring his lunch soon."

I wrote that on the notepad and showed it to James.

"Go ahead and eat." James nodded and smiled.

Judging by their expressions, Billy and Grandpa felt as guilty as I did that we'd be eating without him.

When I'd eaten about half of my burger, a nurse came in with James's lunch, which turned out to be a cup of orange gelatin and some applesauce.

We all stared at it doubtfully.

"Don't worry, dear," the nurse told James. "If you keep this down, I can get you something more substantial later."

I wrote that on the notepad and showed it to him.

"OK," James said, reaching for the fork provided with his food.

The nurse observed James until he finished his food and for a few minutes afterward. When she was satisfied that he had kept it down, she made a note in his chart and left.

Not long after that, a different nurse came in with a wheelchair to take James to his first test.

After they left, we glanced around the room, unsure what to do with ourselves. There was a TV hanging on the wall, so Billy found the remote and started flipping through the channels. He found a marathon of one of those shows where they fix up old houses and sell them, so we all settled onto various uncomfortable pieces of furniture and watched.

They brought James back after about an hour, and

then about thirty minutes later, came and got him for a different test. This pattern continued for most of the afternoon and into the evening. James came and went, but the rest of us stayed in the room: me, Billy, Grandpa, and an elephant the size of a tank. We barely said two words to each other all day, none of us willing to say what we were all thinking.

At about seven, a nurse brought James back to the room for good. Sitting in his wheelchair, my cousin looked completely exhausted. Billy lent James his arm as he climbed into bed. Before I could ask him if he was OK, Dr. Blakely came in.

"We've run all the tests we can for today," he told us. "I've spoken with an audiologist, and he's agreed to come to the hospital tomorrow. You all should try to get some rest." He said the last part mechanically, as if he didn't really care if we followed his advice, and left without another word. He appeared not to have forgiven us for being right about James's condition or for Billy's insults. Maybe both.

James looked at me wearily, wanting to know what the doctor had said. I pulled out the notebook and wrote "Audiologist tomorrow."

He nodded.

"You should all go home and get some sleep," he said, failing at pretending he didn't mind spending the night in the hospital alone.

"I'm staying," Grandpa said, "but you two go on home."

Billy and I looked at each other, outraged, and were about to protest, but Grandpa cut us off.

"Go," he ordered, every inch a Marine drill sergeant.

I heaved a deep sigh. "Yes sir," I said, walking over to give James a hug. "Good night. I love you."

He smiled. "Good night."

"See you in the morning," Billy added as we headed for the door.

The two of us were quiet for the whole ride home. We made good time considering that the elephant from the hospital room was now sitting in the backseat. When we got home, we each made sandwiches. After we ate, we sat at the table, unsure what to do or say.

I felt like the elephant was lying across my chest, and I just couldn't take it anymore. "What if it's permanent, Billy?"

His deep sigh told me he understood exactly what I meant. What if James never heard anything ever again?

"I don't know," Billy said.

Tears filled my eyes just thinking about it. I might never be able to really talk with my cousin again.

"It should've been me," Billy said, shaking his head.

"What?" I asked, bewildered.

"If one of us had to get hurt like this, it should've been me. I play football. I get in fights. I take more risks in a week than James has taken in his whole life. I should be the one this is happening to."

"Billy, that doesn't—"

"Music is his life, Ally. His whole life. He plays three instruments. He sings. He told me a few weeks ago he thought God was calling him into a music ministry." Billy shook his head. "If it were me, it wouldn't matter so much. I could still play football, and I don't have any idea what I want to do after high school. But for James…I just don't know."

I looked down at my lap, suddenly ashamed that I had been thinking selfishly about what this would mean for me instead of what it would mean for James.

Billy stood up and put his plate in the sink. "I'm going to bed."

"It's barely eight o'clock."

He shrugged. "It's been a long day."

As he walked toward his room, a thought struck me. "We should pray together before you go to bed."

He looked at me, eyebrows raised. "With just the two of us?"

"We've never not prayed. It would be a shame to start now."

"All right."

I could tell he was just humoring me.

We knelt across from each other in the living room and each said about a ten-second prayer asking God to heal James. It was pathetic, but since Grandpa and James normally said the longer prayers, it was the best we could muster.

After I said amen, Billy went to his room and shut the door.

I did the same, even though I wasn't ready to go to sleep. Wanting something to distract me from my worries, I grabbed one of my sci-fi novels and reread some of my favorite chapters. Eventually, I got tired, so

I changed into my pajamas without even bothering to shower and crawled into bed. To my surprise, I fell asleep almost instantly.

Billy and I headed to the hospital as soon as we got up the next morning. When we walked onto the third floor, one of the nurses from the previous day told us that James had been moved to a different room because he didn't need to be as closely monitored as before. After checking the computer, she directed us to Room 224.

When we got there, we found Grandpa sitting by himself. He told us the audiologist had already come and taken James for more tests, so Billy and I watched some more episodes of that house-fixing show while we waited.

Grandpa went home to take a shower, but he returned so quickly it was as though he never left.

A nurse brought James back just before lunch. He looked better than he had the previous day, not as peaked and a little steadier on his feet. He was able to move from his wheelchair to the bed by himself. Once he was settled, he watched the show with us.

After a few minutes, Billy knit his brow, looking back and forth between James and the TV. Then, rolling his eyes, he grabbed the remote and turned on the closed captions. I cringed at our thoughtlessness, but James just thanked him and moved on.

The rest of the day passed the same way. Before Billy and I went home that night, Grandpa made us promise to bring our schoolwork to the hospital the next day. Begrudgingly, we obeyed, so Sunday was spent doing homework, rather than watching TV, as James did therapy and had even more tests run.

Around dusk, Dr. Blakely came in. He looked somber, which was ominous. He had never looked anything but miffed when talking to us. Billy took one look at his face and turned off the TV. We all stared at him, waiting for him to speak, as he walked to the foot of James's bed and cleared his throat.

I grabbed a notepad and pen in case I needed to translate.

"The audiologist has finished his tests," he said. "Based on these tests and those from yesterday, we have both come to the same conclusion." He heaved a sigh and looked James straight in the eye. "For the time being, you are profoundly deaf. Because this was the result of an injury, we can't rule out the possibility that you will regain some of your hearing, but more than likely, you need to prepare yourself for this condition to be permanent."

For a few seconds, no one moved. I'm pretty sure we didn't even breathe.

Then James turned to look at me, his eyes pleading, begging me not to confirm what he must have already known to be true.

With shaky hands, I wrote on the notepad. Tears filled my eyes as I turned it around to face him. I'd written just three words: deaf, probably permanent.

7

—HOME IS A FOUR-LETTER WORD

James had to stay in the hospital for a few more days. They did a handful of tests, but mostly they just let him rest and regain his strength. After receiving the news from Dr. Blakely, James was so quiet he could have still been unconscious. He didn't initiate conversation, and when we spoke/wrote to him, he responded as succinctly as possible. The one time Grandpa tried to broach the subject of his hearing loss, James shut him down instantly. None of us knew what to do.

Of course, Grandpa insisted that Billy and I had to go to school that week.

Normally, I would have been really stressed during the week before finals, but I just couldn't bring myself to care. My grades seemed so insignificant compared to what James was facing. I spent my time at school wishing I was at the hospital and telling people that James had woken up and was doing better whenever they asked.

On Tuesday evening, I was sitting in James's hospital room, solving a page of quadratic equations, when a doctor I'd never seen entered the room carrying a small white board, a dry erase marker, and some pamphlets. He was in his forties with salt and pepper hair and kind eyes.

"How are you doing today, James?" he asked. He had the same question written on the white board that he held up for James to read.

I stared at him, trying to figure out if I knew this man since he obviously knew James.

"That's Dr. Snowden, the audiologist," Grandpa whispered, seeing my confusion.

"I'm all right, I guess," James replied. Thankfully, he was wearing a hospital gown. If he had pants on, they probably would've spontaneously combusted. *Liar, liar....*

The audiologist just nodded. From the look on his face, he knew exactly what James really meant. "I brought you these," he said, handing the pamphlets to James. "They talk about the different ways people with a hearing loss communicate. Read through them tonight, and I'll discuss them with you in the morning." He wrote that on the dry erase board as well.

"Thank you," James said, setting the pamphlets in his lap without even glancing at them.

"You can go home tomorrow," Dr. Snowden said and wrote.

"I can?"

"He can?" Grandpa asked, sounding as surprised as James.

The audiologist nodded. "Dr. Blakely and I discussed it." He glanced back at James, wrote on the white board again, and then held it up for him to see as he said, "Your life isn't over. It's just changing." He handed me the white board and marker and then looked at Grandpa. "Mr. Griffin, could I speak to you in the hallway?"

After Grandpa followed Dr. Snowden out the door, James looked down at the pamphlets for a few seconds before shoving them aside. He kept his head lowered, but I'm pretty sure tears glistened in his eyes. Once again, I wanted to wrap my arms around him and tell him it would be all right. Three things stopped me. First, I knew he would probably push me away. Second, he wouldn't hear me tell him anything while I was hugging him. And third, I wasn't sure it was true.

At eight, Grandpa insisted that Billy and I go home so we could get a good night's sleep before school the next day. We both tried to convince him to let us skip school so we could be there when James got home. Grandpa wouldn't even consider it.

James was released from the hospital on Wednesday morning. I spent the entire school day distracted, and when the bell finally rang for dismissal, I practically sprinted for the bus.

"Ally, is everything OK?" Missy asked, sitting down next to me. "You seem really on edge today."

I didn't answer immediately.

"Did something happen with James?"

For a moment, I hesitated, but when I saw the compassion in Missy's eyes, the truth came tumbling out of my lips.

"Wow," Missy said when I was done. "That's a lot to deal with. How's James handling being deaf?"

"I don't know," I told her honestly. "He won't talk about it."

She knit her brow. "This will be really hard for him. For all of you." She studied my face. "How are *you* handling it?"

"I don't think it's sunk in yet," I replied. "I just can't seem to wrap my mind around the fact that this is actually happening."

"I'm really sorry. I'll be praying for all of you. Let me know if there's anything else I can do."

I told her I would, knowing in my heart there never would be.

When Billy and I got off the bus, my stomach started fluttering. I'd wanted to be home all day, but now I was scared stiff. I didn't know how to act around James. Should I talk to him normally? Should I not talk to him at all? Should I carry a notepad and pen at all times and write to him?

The audiologist had given James a number of pamphlets about how to deal with his hearing loss. Why hadn't he given us one about how to deal with a family member's hearing loss? We were in uncharted territory without so much as a pamphlet for guidance. Sure, we'd communicated and interacted with James in the hospital, but that was different. No one knows exactly how they're supposed to act in a hospital, so it's OK if it's awkward. But this was home, the place I'd always been the most comfortable, and I had no idea what I was supposed to do. Just before we walked onto the porch, Billy looked over at me, and I could tell he was feeling the same way.

"It'll be OK," he said.

I couldn't tell if he was telling himself or me. "Of course," I said, though I didn't believe it for a second.

Together, we braced ourselves and walked inside where we found Grandpa in the kitchen cooking supper.

"Where's James?" Billy asked as we both scanned the portion of the house we could see.

"He went for a walk. How was school?"

"Fine," we said in unison.

"How's he doing?" I asked.

Grandpa shrugged. "He seems all right." He took the lid off a pot and stirred it but didn't elaborate.

Billy glowered at him. "James came home from the hospital this morning after losing his hearing, and all you have to say is that he went for a walk and he seems all right?"

Grandpa put the lid back on the pot and turned toward us. "What else do you want to know?"

"I don't know," Billy said, "but more than that."

Grandpa considered that for a moment. "First thing this morning, Dr. Snowden talked to us about different ways that people with a hearing loss communicate. Of the options he gave, James was most interested in learning to speech read, and—"

"Speech read?" I interrupted. "Is that different from lip reading?"

"I asked the same thing," Grandpa said. "Dr. Snowden said that speech reading is a more accurate term because it includes things like body language, too."

I nodded. That made sense.

"He also said that developing speech reading skills takes time, so if James doesn't understand what we say the first time, we might need to write it down." He peeked inside the oven.

"After Dr. Snowden left, Dr. Blakely came by and gave James a final checkup. He said that James can do anything he feels like doing, but that he shouldn't push himself for a few days. Then we checked out and came home. He has a follow-up appointment with Dr. Snowden in a few weeks." He paused. "What else is there?"

"How is James handling being deaf?" I asked. "Is he upset?"

Grandpa sighed. "Probably, but when I asked, he said he didn't want to talk about it. The doctor told me to take my cues from him, so I haven't forced him to."

"So, what are we supposed to do?" I demanded. "Pretend nothing has changed?"

Grandpa didn't answer right away. He stirred the pot on the stove, looking thoughtful.

I was ready to snatch the spoon from his hand and demand answers, but Grandpa finally looked at us. "James has an appointment with a therapist in a couple weeks. It's someone the audiologist recommended for those dealing with a sensory loss. Hopefully, she'll help him work through…whatever he needs to work through. When push comes to shove, though, James will have to deal with this on his own. All we can do is be there for him."

I was glad the audiologist had referred James to a

therapist and hoped that talking to her would help him come to terms with his hearing loss. But Grandpa still hadn't answered my question. I tried to think of a way to rephrase what I wanted to know, but Billy beat me to it.

"What are we supposed to do right now?" he asked. "Tonight, tomorrow, and however long?"

"The best we can," Grandpa said. "James said that he doesn't want me to treat him any different, so I'm doing my best not to. I've been talking to him normally. If he doesn't understand what I say the first time, I repeat it. He seems to like that better than me writing it down." He took the chicken he was baking out of the oven.

"That's it?" I asked.

"For now. I'm sure he'll need more than that from us eventually. We'll just have to play it by ear."

Billy grimaced. "Poor choice of words, Grandpa, but I know what you mean."

Grandpa shook his head at himself. Then he looked at us, his eyes level. "Enough talking. You two need to go do your homework."

"Yes sir," we both said automatically and went to our rooms to do just that.

I stayed in my room for the rest of the afternoon, double checking all of my homework and getting a head start on studying for my finals the next week. I told myself that I was just being studious, but deep down, I knew I wanted to avoid running into James. I felt like a horrible cousin, but I just didn't know what to say to him.

Grandpa called us to the table for supper, so I went to the kitchen, fixed myself a plate, and sat down. Grandpa was already sitting at the head of the table, and Billy was piling his plate with noodles. But James was nowhere to be seen.

"Where's James?" I asked.

Grandpa frowned. "He was sitting on the porch studying. Surely, he heard me yell..." He winced and left the statement unfinished.

Billy set his mountain of noodles on the table. "I'll get him," he said and walked out the door. A few seconds later, he came back with James on his heels.

James surveyed the room. When his shoulders sagged slightly, I could tell he knew he'd missed the call to dinner. Before I could think of anything to say to make him feel better, he started fixing his plate, trying to hide his embarrassment.

As soon as James was seated, Grandpa bowed his head and began saying the blessing as he usually did. I closed my eyes, not wanting to seem irreverent, but as Grandpa thanked God for James being home, a thought occurred to me. James couldn't close his eyes if he wanted to know what was going on. I opened my eyes.

Sure enough, James had his eyes open, watching Grandpa intently. Following his gaze, I stifled a groan. With his head bowed, Grandpa's mustache completely obscured his lips, making it impossible for James to have any idea what he was saying.

Pursing my lips, I closed my eyes and tried to focus on Grandpa's words, rather than my cousin's predicament. A minute later, Grandpa said amen and started eating without ever realizing James had been completely excluded from the blessing. I decided now wasn't the time to point it out.

"So how was school today?" James asked.

I swallowed a mouthful of spaghetti. "All right," I said with a shrug.

"Not too bad," Billy said at almost the same time.

James nodded, his eyes on me, and then turned to look at Billy, who was focusing so intently on his supper that he didn't notice. With as little movement as possible, I kicked him under the table.

Billy looked up, surprised, and saw James looking at him, still expecting an answer. "Not too bad," Billy repeated before turning his attention back to his spaghetti. My oldest cousin could put away some carbohydrates.

"That's good," James said and turned his attention to his food as well.

No one said anything for the rest of the meal. Only when we were all finished did Billy reach over and tap James on the shoulder. "A lot of people at school are asking about you. What do you want us to tell them?"

James stared at him for several seconds and then seemed to realize he was waiting for a response. "I'm sorry. What?"

"School," Billy said slowly.

James nodded.

"What do you"—he pointed to James—"want us,"—he gestured to himself and me—"to tell people about you?" He pointed at James again.

James heaved a sigh. "People are asking about me?"

Billy nodded, looking relieved not to have to repeat himself again.

"Tell them the truth," James said after a moment. "Tell them I can't hear."

"Are you sure?" I asked him.

He didn't answer.

Billy jerked his head in my direction, and James looked at me.

"Are you sure?" I repeated before he could apologize for not hearing me.

He nodded. "They'll find out eventually anyway. Maybe if you tell them now, they can get used to the idea over the summer."

Billy gave him a thumbs-up. "You got it," he said, not seeming concerned at all.

I wished I could feel the same way.

"Speaking of school," James said, looking at Grandpa. "I'd like to go tomorrow."

"What?" all three of us said, staring at him as if he'd lost his mind.

"I don't want to go to my classes," he explained quickly. "But I thought maybe you could go with me and talk to my teachers about letting me make up my work and take my exams next week. And...we also need to start thinking about next year."

I could tell it was hard for him to say that last part, to admit that things would have to be different next year.

Grandpa gazed at him thoughtfully and then

nodded. "I'll call the school tomorrow morning and see if we can schedule a meeting with your teachers."

I'm not sure if James caught any of what Grandpa said, but his nod was clear enough.

"Thanks, Grandpa," James said.

"You're welcome," Grandpa said, standing up and taking his dishes to the sink. The rest of us followed.

We showered in our usual order that night. I considered offering to let James go before me but decided against it. Grandpa had said he wanted to be treated normally, which for him, meant showering last.

When we were all ready for bed, Grandpa called us to the living room to pray, so I set down my book and headed that way. Fortunately, Billy and James had been in their room together, so Billy was able to relay Grandpa's message to James. At least, I assumed that was what happened because they both came to the living room together.

The four of us knelt in a circle as we always did. Grandpa prayed first. I opened my eyes shortly after he started, expecting to see his lips hidden behind his mustache again. Instead, I found that Grandpa's head was only slightly bowed, leaving his lips clearly visible. With a small smile, I bowed my head. Apparently, Grandpa hadn't been as oblivious as I'd thought.

That night, Grandpa's prayer was longer than usual (which was saying something). When he finished, the rest of us each said a short one of our own. During my prayer, I made sure to bow my head only slightly and not to speak too fast. Although I wasn't brave enough to open my eyes to check, I was pretty sure Billy did the same. He definitely enunciated each word clearly. After we all prayed, I went back to my room and went to sleep, grateful the long day was finally over.

The next day at school was hard. Some of my teachers and a few students asked about James, so I was forced to tell them about his hearing loss. Most of them didn't know how to respond. They just mumbled something about being sorry and walked away. I spent the day feeling awkward and stressed. It was a relief to get on the bus and head home, until I remembered that I didn't know how to act around James once I got there.

When Billy and I walked up to the house, Grandpa was sitting on the porch. He greeted us with a smile.

"How did it go with James's teachers?" Billy asked without preamble.

My shoulders sagged. With all the questions I'd had to field at school, I'd forgotten all about Grandpa arranging a meeting with James's teachers.

"Fine," Grandpa said. "They all agreed to exempt James from the assignments he missed and to let him take his finals in the front office."

"Good," I said, swallowing my guilt. I glanced around. "Where's James?"

"In his room," Grandpa replied. "He said that since he missed two weeks of material, he needs to start studying for his finals now."

Billy grimaced. "I bet he does."

I nodded in agreement, doing my best to hide my

relief. If James was focused on studying, it meant I would probably only have to interact with him at mealtimes and during our nightly prayers for the next week. By the time finals were over, I was sure I'd feel more comfortable around him. After all, I loved my cousin dearly, and nothing would keep me from communicating with him for long.

As I expected, the next week passed in a blur of books, note cards, and test questions, interrupted by the occasional awkward meal or prayer time. At last, Thursday afternoon came, and finals were over. Grandpa made jambalaya for dinner to celebrate, and we were excited enough to forget our nervousness and actually talk as we ate.

From the glances I stole from the corner of my eye, I could tell James couldn't really follow most of the conversation, but he didn't seem to mind that much. He looked relieved to see us behaving as we usually did, and I let myself hope that maybe things would start getting back to normal.

That night, I went to bed fairly early, exhausted but excited that it was finally summer. At about two in the morning, I woke up to the sound of someone screaming at the top of their lungs. Disoriented, I sat up in bed, trying to figure out what was going on. After a second, I realized it was James's voice, so I jumped out of bed and ran into the living room where I met Grandpa coming out of the hall. Together, we rushed to Billy and James's closed door. The light was on in their room, and the screaming stopped just before Grandpa opened the door.

"What happened? Are you all right?" Grandpa asked as I followed him into the room.

James was sitting up in bed breathing hard, his eyes rimmed with terror.

Billy was sitting on the edge of James's bed, intentionally putting his face in James's line of sight. His back was to us. "It's OK," Billy said slowly, pointing at his lips. "You're OK."

James reached up and touched one of his ears, as though he was trying to remove whatever was blocking the sound. Then he looked down at his lap and let his hand fall. After taking a couple of deep breaths, he looked up at Billy, his fear replaced by sorrow and resignation.

Billy nodded and stood up, turning to face us. "We're fine," he told Grandpa, although his face said otherwise.

James's brow furrowed as he studied Grandpa and me, trying to figure out why we were there.

"Did I wake you up?" he asked.

Grandpa hesitated, but I nodded, not wanting to make him feel bad, but sure that he'd want the truth.

"I'm sorry," he said.

"It's OK," I told him. "Are you all right?"

"I'm fine. Just a nightmare."

I wasn't sure if he'd read my lips or the concern in my eyes.

"Do you want to talk about it?" Grandpa asked.

James didn't even notice he'd spoken. "You can go back to bed."

Grandpa nodded, and we both left without

another word. It took a long time for me to fall asleep after that. I couldn't quite shake the image of James's terrified face as he woke up to something worse than his nightmare.

The next morning, James ate his breakfast in silence. After he put away his dishes, he mumbled another apology for waking us up and went to take a walk.

"I'm sorry," Billy said as soon as the door shut behind James.

"For what?" I asked, mystified.

Grandpa raised his eyebrows, seemingly as confused as I was.

"James was tossing and turning quite a bit before he screamed. I should've woken him up sooner."

Grandpa shook his head. "It wasn't your fault."

Billy stared at his cereal. "He's had nightmares before. Not often, but several times I can remember. All I ever had to do was say his name a few times, and he'd wake up." He rubbed his face. "I tried that for a minute last night before I remembered he couldn't hear me, and even then, I didn't want to get out of bed to wake him up. I waited a minute to see if he would stop on his own. That's when he started screaming."

I rolled my eyes. "No one likes getting out of bed in the middle of the night, Billy. You didn't do anything wrong."

He nodded, still looking unconvinced. "Well, next time, if there is a next time, I'll wake him up faster…and more carefully."

I raised my eyebrows at him.

"He hit me," he explained, taking a bite of cereal.

"What?" Grandpa asked.

I would have asked too, but my mouth was full.

"Not on purpose," Billy said. "When I shook him to wake him up, that was his first reaction. I could've dodged if I'd been expecting it, but he caught me off guard." He shrugged like it wasn't important.

"He hit you?" I was still stunned. "Where?"

"Across the jaw," Billy said, rubbing his face. "He's got a decent right cross."

I must have still looked incredulous because Billy laughed. "Don't look so shocked, Ally. It's not as if he was trying to hurt me. It was just a reflex. He doesn't even remember doing it."

"He doesn't?" I asked.

"No. He would've apologized a million times if he remembered, and he hasn't mentioned it once."

"Will you tell him?" I asked. It seemed like a reasonable question. I'd want someone to know if they punched me.

"No." Billy acted as if the idea was absurd. "Why would I? Then he'd feel bad about something he couldn't control. He does that enough as it is." He shook his head. "So, what do you want us to do today, Grandpa?"

"Why don't you relax today?" Grandpa said with a smile, making us both eye him suspiciously. That question was so out of character for him that it belonged in a different book.

"I'll give you one day of freedom," he said. "Tomorrow, we'll start catching up on all the things that need to be done around here."

I smiled. That was the Grandpa I knew and loved...and only occasionally resented.

After picking out one of my favorite books, I sat on the porch and read all day. Except for meals, I spent hours wonderfully oblivious to what the rest of my family was doing.

Before we went to bed that night, Grandpa said he wanted all of us ready to work by eight o'clock the next morning. I thought that was pretty ridiculous for the first Saturday of the summer but wisely decided to keep that opinion to myself. As I lay in bed that night, I couldn't help but feel a little anxious. What if James had another nightmare and woke us all up again? Thankfully, my fear proved groundless.

When my alarm went off in the morning, I glared at it resentfully and stayed in bed another fifteen minutes. Then I forced myself to get up. On my way to the kitchen, I heard Billy saying "Time to get up" with exaggerated enunciation. Pausing outside their door, I tried to figure out why he was waking James up until it dawned on me that he couldn't hear an alarm clock. Shaking my head at my own cluelessness, I walked to the kitchen.

As I ate my breakfast, I wondered how deaf people woke themselves up in the morning. Surely, they didn't all have someone shake or tap them. I decided I'd research it the next time I had Internet access—which wouldn't be for a while.

Just as Grandpa had ordered, Billy, James, and I were all ready to work at eight o'clock sharp. We sat at the kitchen table, bleary-eyed, waiting to be assigned our duties.

Grandpa, who always woke up before sunrise, came inside and smiled at us cheerfully. "Good morning, sleepyheads," he said, suppressing a chuckle.

"Morning, Grandpa," we all muttered.

"Billy, you'll be weeding today," he said, getting straight to the point. "The garden is in a sad state."

Billy nodded without enthusiasm. When Grandpa wasn't around, he referred to weeding as the chore that never ends using the tune to a song from an old kids' show.

"Ally, you'll be helping him."

"Yes sir," I said, trying to hide my surprise.

During the summer, I hardly ever worked in the garden. Sometimes, I helped with the harvest in the fall, particularly when more than one vegetable was ripe at the same time, but it had been years since I'd weeded. Grandpa normally asked Billy and James to do the harder outdoor labor and let me do the indoor, porch, and barn chores. There were more than enough of those to keep me busy.

"James, you'll gather the eggs," Grandpa said. "When you finish, you can clean the kitchen." He handed him a post-it with his chores listed on it, in case he hadn't understood.

"Yes, sir," James said without looking at it.

"Let's get to work." Grandpa headed back outside.

When he was gone, James looked at the post-it and frowned. "These are your chores, Ally."

"Not today." I shook my head for emphasis.

James pursed his lips. "I'm not an invalid."

"He's just worried about you, James," I told him.

He frowned. I couldn't tell if he'd understood me, but he knew I agreed with Grandpa's decision.

"It was one time," he argued. "I won't collapse every time I step out the door."

"It's only been two weeks, James," Billy said.

"What?" James snapped. He closed his eyes and took a deep breath. "I'm sorry," he said in a softer tone.

Billy shrugged one shoulder, unfazed. It would take a lot more than that to bother him. He picked up the post-it and wrote "2 weeks."

James read it and nodded.

"Give him time," Billy added, pointing vaguely in Grandpa's direction and then to his wrist.

"I know." James sighed.

I tapped him on the shoulder. "You scared us," I told him. "We didn't know if…we thought you might…" I couldn't bring myself to say it. I blinked back tears.

James's expression softened. He hugged me, the first real hug he'd given me since he woke up. Then he held me at arms' length. "I'm OK. Well, except for the obvious." He turned to look at Billy. "The holes in the barn roof still need to be patched. Grandpa won't ask you to do it because you never take the time to test them thoroughly. Now he won't let me do it. So who do you think will do it?"

Billy sighed, and I gnawed my lower lip.

We all knew who would do it: Grandpa. A sixty-six-year-old man on a barn roof in one-hundred-degree heat. What could possibly go wrong?

"He'll kill himself trying to protect me," James warned.

"I'll talk to him," Billy said, pointing at himself.

James looked relieved. "And I'll do the woman's work for today," he said, giving me a half-smile to let me know he was joking.

With all of that settled, we headed outside.

Sure enough, Grandpa was on top of the barn patching holes.

James rolled his eyes and walked toward the chicken coop.

I gave Billy an encouraging nod and started weeding the row closest to the barn, hoping I would be able to hear his conversation with Grandpa.

Billy cast me an annoyed look to let me know my eavesdropping was getting old. He started climbing the ladder Grandpa had used to get onto the roof. "What are you doing?" Billy asked as he made his way up.

"What does it look like?" Grandpa asked.

Billy reached the roof and scowled. "Something dangerous. It's too hot for you to be up here. And you're too...well...too old to be doing this."

"That's ridiculous," Grandpa told him. "I was patching roofs before you were born."

Billy gave him a look. "You know you just proved my point, right?"

"You know what I mean," Grandpa snapped and bent down to start working again.

"Grandpa, I know why you're doing this. But you

have to stop. It's not safe. I know I've never really had the patience for patching, but I'll try if you want me to. Or better yet, wait a week or two and let James do it."

Grandpa started to protest.

Billy cut him off. "I'll help him. We'll take a lot of breaks and drink plenty of water. No one will get overheated. It'll be fine. Now, will you please come down?"

Grandpa stroked his mustache. "What if we have a big storm this week?" he asked.

"That's what buckets are for," Billy said. "Please, Grandpa, come down."

Grandpa stared at the sky, his brow furrowed, and finally nodded. "All right," he said and headed for the ladder.

Billy grabbed the roof-patching supplies and followed him down, looking as relieved as I felt. Neither of us had expected it to be that easy.

Billy and I weeded for the rest of the day. The weeds had grown practically unchecked for three weeks, and the garden was all but overgrown. We took a lunch break around noon and stopped several times to go inside and drink water. When Grandpa told us we could stop around dinner time, I stood up and felt sweat trickle down my aching back. It had been a very long day.

Billy looked at me and smiled mischievously as he wiped the sweat from his brow. "This is the chore that never ends," he sang.

"Shut up," I told him. "That was exhausting. I will be so glad when James can work out here again."

Billy's smile faded. "I don't know when that'll be. I convinced Grandpa to come down this morning, but it was a near thing. And I know he wasn't sold on the idea of James patching the roof, even with my help."

"Can you blame him?" I asked. "James could've died in that accident. If you hadn't caught him—"

"But I did," Billy interrupted firmly.

"I know. But what if it happens again? You might not be there the next time."

Billy stopped walking and turned to look me in the eye. "Look, I know how close we came to losing him, all right? I've had a few nightmares of my own about what would've happened if I didn't get to him in time. But I did, and he's fine. Deaf, but fine."

I shook my head stubbornly. "He still needs to be careful."

"He will be," Billy said. "We'll all make sure of that."

"But—"

"He needs this, Ally," Billy said. "Couldn't you see it in his eyes this morning? He needs to feel as though he's still contributing around here."

I narrowed my eyes. "He did what would normally be my chores. Are you saying I don't contribute?"

"No. I'm saying he doesn't feel as if he's doing the most he can, and he's right." He glanced around at the garden. "If James had been working with me today, we would've finished weeding."

I turned away angrily and stalked toward the house. That was uncalled for.

"I wasn't trying to insult you," Billy placated.

I froze but didn't turn around.

"I was just making a point. We each a have a...a...niche we fill around here. James is deaf now, so there are a lot of things he can't do anymore. But he can still do his outside chores. Can't you see why he wants to?"

My shoulders slumped. I hated to admit it, but Billy had a point. James wanted things to be as normal as possible, and working outside was what he normally did. And he could still do it. We just had to let him.

Billy walked up beside me. "I'm worried about him, too, but treating him as though he's delicate will only make him mad."

"My head knows you're right. My heart just doesn't want to accept it."

"There seems to be a lot of that going around," he said and started walking toward the house again.

I frowned, knowing he was referring to Grandpa. I wondered if I could do something about that. Then I headed for the house as well. "What's a niche?" I asked Billy's retreating back.

"The specific role an organism fulfills in an ecosystem," he said.

I stopped walking. "What?"

"Oh, give me a break," he said. "I spent half of this week studying for my biology exam. It just popped into my head."

"Wow, that's—"

"Shut up!"

Giggling, I followed him onto the porch.

He opened the door, stepped into the kitchen, and stopped so abruptly that I almost ran into him.

"What's the matter with you?" I demanded, walking around him.

Then I saw what he was staring at. The kitchen was immaculate. There wasn't a dirty dish or speck of food to be seen, and all the flat surfaces, including the floor, gleamed. James's patient and meticulous nature had certainly been put to good use.

"I take back everything I just told you," Billy said. "James needs to stay inside for at least a week…or however long it'll take him to clean the rest of the house."

I elbowed him playfully, knowing he had a point. When I cleaned the kitchen, it ended up clean, not spotless.

James walked in from the living room and eyed us curiously. "What are you looking at?"

"Our shiny kitchen," Billy said, walking toward the living room. "Nice work, Clean Machine."

"What did he say?" James asked.

"It's not important," I told him, rolling my eyes. "I'm going to take a shower."

James nodded, looking unconvinced, and wandered out to the porch. Concerned, I looked out the window over the sink and saw him collapse into a rocking chair. He put his hands over his face, breathing hard. I hurried away from the window to make sure he didn't know I'd seen him.

James hadn't understood a word Billy had said,

and I'd just brushed aside his request for clarification as though it was nothing. I hadn't meant to be inconsiderate. Billy's joke just hadn't seemed worth repeating.

I rubbed my face with my hands. That wasn't my call to make. I needed to make sure I remembered that.

Still, what were we supposed to do? Not talk to each other when he was around? Write down every word we said in his presence? I sighed deeply as I headed toward the bathroom to take a shower, wondering how any of us could ever be comfortable at home if we couldn't communicate.

8

—DEAFNESS IS SILENCING

Since I felt as though I'd let James down by not repeating Billy's joke, I desperately wanted to do something, anything, to help him. The more I thought about it, the more I knew what I had to do. Billy was right. James needed to be allowed to do his outdoor chores. He needed to know that there was something in his life that hadn't changed. Grandpa was the only one who could let him, and I knew if anyone could convince him, it would be me. I was the youngest and the only girl. When I wanted to, I could convince Grandpa of almost anything. Besides that, I knew exactly how he felt.

Grandpa went to sit on the porch after supper, so I steeled my nerves and joined him. I tried desperately to think of a way to start a conversation that would naturally come around to the topic I wanted to discuss. Since nothing came to mind, we sat and listened to the crickets.

Grandpa looked over at me. "What's on your mind, baby?" he asked.

I smiled at how well he knew me. "Why did you have James do my chores today?"

He met my gaze with knowing eyes. "You know

117

why."

I nodded. I did know why, and part of me agreed with him. But this wasn't about me. It was about James. I swallowed hard and made myself continue. "James was upset that you didn't let him do his normal chores."

Grandpa sighed. "I was afraid he might be, but it was the best option I could think of."

I took a deep breath, praying the Lord would give me the right words to help him understand. "I know why you don't want him working outside. But I think it's doing more harm than good. James wants things to be as normal as possible. You're the one who told us that."

"I know. But it's only been a week and a half since he got out of the hospital. It's too soon for him to be out in the heat again."

Yes, it is, my heart agreed firmly. *Is that really your call?* a voice in my mind countered. It sounded a lot like Billy.

"Don't you think James would be a better judge of that than you are?" I asked, trying to make my voice as gentle as possible.

Grandpa stared at me, and for just a moment, I could see the immeasurable grief he'd experienced in his life. The loss of his wife and so many others. I saw his fear of losing someone else just as dear.

He reached over and squeezed my hand. "You're right," he said softly, "and I'll try to remember that next time."

I squeezed back. "Me, too."

Billy chose that moment to walk out of the house.

"Grandpa, where—" He froze when he saw us holding hands, tears in both our eyes. "I can come back later." He started to turn around.

I let go of Grandpa's hand. "We were finished anyway." I stood up. "He's all yours, Billy."

As I walked back inside, I felt some measure of peace, knowing that I had done what I could to help James, even if he never knew it.

Exhausted, physically and emotionally, I spent the rest of the evening reading in my room, coming out only to shower and pray as a family. I was planning to go straight back there the moment I said amen.

But Grandpa asked Billy and me to come to the kitchen for a minute. Puzzled, we did as he asked.

"I wanted to let you know that James won't be coming to church with us tomorrow," Grandpa said as soon as the door swung shut. "We talked about it, and he wants to wait until next week."

"Probably a good idea," Billy said. "It'll give us a chance to tell everyone about him losing his hearing."

I cringed, already dreading it.

Grandpa studied me. "I know it's hard, baby. But the more people we tell, the fewer James will have to."

"I know you're right. It's just so awkward sometimes."

Billy smiled at me. "Don't worry about it, Ally. I'll tell Lee, and he'll make an announcement to the youth group during Sunday school. You probably won't have to tell anyone."

I smiled back at him, relieved.

"Well, that's settled." Grandpa yawned. "You two can go to bed."

I walked to my room and crawled into bed, wondering when this would get easier.

Sunday went about as well as possible. We got to church a little early, so Billy was able to talk to Lee before everyone else arrived. Lee made the announcement during Sunday school, and other than a collective gasp, no one said anything about it.

Apparently, Grandpa had asked Pastor Benjamin to do the same thing during the church service because he announced it to the congregation while he was listing the prayer concerns for the week.

Just as Billy predicted, I didn't have to personally deliver the news to anyone, for which I was profoundly grateful.

On Monday, Grandpa drove James to Monroe for his appointment with the therapist. Knowing the two of them would be gone all morning, Billy and I used that time to continue weeding the garden. We took a lunch break at noon, and Grandpa and James got back while we were still eating. They joined us at the table but didn't say much.

When we were finished, James looked at Grandpa. "Do you mind if I go for a walk?"

I tried to hide my surprise. Billy and I had clearly been working outside all morning. Normally, James would have felt obligated to join us, or at least to do chores inside if Grandpa wouldn't let him. What on earth had the therapist said to him?

"That's fine," Grandpa replied with a nod, so

James put his plate in the sink and left.

Billy and I stared at Grandpa quizzically.

"Don't look at me," Grandpa said. "That's the first time he's initiated conversation since we left Monroe. I tried to ask him about his appointment on the way back, but he said he was tired, and then pretended to sleep."

We didn't see much of James for the rest of the day. He alternated between walking in the woods and sequestering himself in his room, so the rest of us alternated between looking concerned and pretending not to notice.

On Tuesday morning, James was more himself. He was in the kitchen with Billy and me at eight on the dot. Grandpa assigned Billy to work in the garden again, and after a slight hesitation, he told James to help him.

I smiled at Grandpa as he told me to gather the eggs and clean the living room, and he smiled back. When we all took a break for lunch, I could tell James was glad to be back in his niche.

Grandpa let James work outside for the rest of the week. By Friday, he was ready to let him and Billy finish patching the roof of the barn. He kept a close eye on them and had me take them water several times, but he let them finish the job. I was immensely proud of him.

James went to church with us the following Sunday, although I got the distinct impression that he didn't want to. He did his best to avoid conversing with anyone during Sunday school and then waited until the service was about to start before joining us in the sanctuary. He stood silently while the rest of the congregation sang hymns and sat rigidly beside me during the sermon. To his credit, he at least pretended to pay attention, even though he couldn't possibly have understood what Pastor Benjamin was saying from so far away. He also kept his eyes open during the prayers to make sure he knew when the person said amen.

When the service was over, we headed for the car as fast as we could, but a number of people still stopped us.

James shook their hands and even let one elderly woman hug him, all the while keeping his face blank.

When we got in the car, his shoulders sagged.

"I'm glad that's over," he said softly and gave us a tired smile. "It went OK, right?"

We all assured him it had.

Grandpa drove James to Monroe to see the therapist again the following Monday. Apparently, she wanted to see him weekly for the rest of the summer. Billy started summer football practice that morning too, so I was left to my own devices. I used the time to finish reading my book.

The summer kind of took on a rhythm after that. Billy was gone for a couple hours every weekday morning for practice. Grandpa decided it wasn't fair to make two of us do more of the work, so we waited until after lunch to start our chores. Grandpa took James to Monroe on Mondays, and we all went to church together on Sundays.

Of course, this pattern was interrupted occasionally. Billy went out with his friends fairly often, and I spent the night at Missy's a couple of times.

James went for his follow-up appointment with Dr. Snowden, who informed him that since his hearing hadn't improved at all, it was almost guaranteed that it never would. That wasn't a surprise, but it was still disappointing.

By unspoken consent, Billy and I didn't invite anyone to our house, knowing James deserved a place where he didn't have to deal with anyone but us.

For the first few weeks, I held out hope that life might truly come close to getting back to normal sometime soon. Then, things began to change.

James started going for walks by himself a lot more often, and he stayed away longer. He gave up trying to talk to us unless it was absolutely necessary and almost never asked us to repeat things.

One day while I was emptying the kitchen trashcan, I found his piano sheet music torn to pieces. When I mentioned it to Billy, he told me he'd found the remains of James's guitar behind the barn, smashed and broken. None of us knew how to help him.

One Sunday in early July, James took a walk right after lunch.

We watched him leave, all with varying concerned expressions. When he was gone, I turned and stared helplessly at Grandpa.

"I know this is hard, baby," he said. "I've decided I'll talk with his therapist tomorrow to see if there's anything we can do to support him. I'll let you know what she says."

"Thanks, Grandpa," I said, sincerely hoping that she could give him some suggestions.

Grandpa and James went to Monroe on Monday morning as usual. When they came back, we all ate lunch together, and then James left for yet another walk.

As soon as he was out the door, I looked at Grandpa expectantly, but he didn't say anything. The three of us sat in silence for what felt like an eternity.

Finally, Billy couldn't take it anymore. "Would you like me to cough suggestively?" he asked Grandpa with more than a hint of impatience.

I glared at him.

"No, Billy," Grandpa said. "I was just trying to decide where to start. The therapist told me a lot, so I guess I should just start at the beginning. She says that losing a sense is kind of like losing a loved one. The person has to grieve for the lost sense before they can learn how to live without it. The grieving process has five stages that often overlap. The first is denial, which James already went through. The second is anger, and according to Dr. Simmons, James is stuck there."

"Stuck?" I repeated. "How did he get stuck in the anger phase?"

"By suppressing it," Grandpa said. "He's holding it all inside, trying to pretend it doesn't exist."

"Why?" Billy and I asked together.

"The therapist wasn't sure," Grandpa said, "but I think it's because he doesn't want to hurt our feelings."

I felt my brow knit in confusion. Hurt our feelings? Why would he hurt our feelings unless... Comprehension darted through me.

"You're not saying he's angry *at us*?" I asked, shocked.

Grandpa sighed. "Well, not at us exactly, but if he were to express his anger, it would probably be directed at us."

I was still confused.

Apparently, so was Billy. "Why would he direct his anger at us?" he asked.

Grandpa ran a hand down his face. "Look, you two were so young when your parents died that you don't really remember what it feels like to lose someone. But I've lost a lot of people I love. I know what that anger feels like. When you're angry at the whole situation, you lash out at random people. You know they don't deserve it, but the anger just bursts out of you anyway. After your grandma died, I yelled at the preacher when he told me God would be there for me. After the car accident that killed your parents and my other grandchildren, I threw a garden rake at our neighbor when he tried to tell me it would be OK."

"You threw a rake at Mr. Francis?" I asked.

"No, at Mr. Codwaller. But that's not the point. I was angry at them for not feeling the pain I was in, for having the nerve to try to help when they couldn't begin to understand what I was going through." Grandpa heaved a sigh.

"So basically, James is angry that he's deaf, and any time something reminds him of that, it makes his anger boil over at whoever is nearby," Billy concluded.

"Exactly," Grandpa said. "It's a normal part of grief, but James won't let it out. He knows it's not fair to us, so he's holding it all inside. That's the problem."

"So, you want James to express his anger at us?" I asked, making air quotes with my hands.

"Yes," Grandpa replied. "It's the only way for him to accept his deafness."

I closed my eyes to stop the tears from coming, trying to imagine what it would be like for James to yell at me for things I couldn't control or change. I shuddered. James had never yelled at me. Grandpa sometimes yelled when I did something wrong, and Billy had lost his temper with me so many times I'd lost count. But to have James do it...

Billy interrupted my thoughts. "Let me make sure I have this straight. James is suppressing his anger at this whole situation, and the only way for him to move on in the grieving process is for him to express it?"

"A very good summary," Grandpa told him.

Billy nodded. "Well, all right then." He stood and walked toward the door with the look in his eyes that meant he was about to take action.

"Billy, what are you going to do?" I asked, remembering where that look had led him in the past.

"Get James to express his anger." He looked me in the eyes.

"By doing what?"

"Whatever it takes."

"I'm coming," I told him, starting to follow.

"No. That'll just make it harder for him. Stay

here." He thought for a second. "Why don't you make sure the hose is attached to the water spigot at the back of the house and bring some towels outside?" He grabbed the door handle.

"You're going to make James fight?" I asked, alarmed.

"Maybe," Billy said. "Depends just how much pressure he's built up inside."

"But you could hurt each other. Forget towels. Maybe I should have the car ready to go to the hospital."

"Ally, stop it," Billy said. "No one will get hurt, at least not seriously."

"But—"

"But nothing. James isn't a good enough fighter to hurt me, and I certainly have no intention of hurting him."

"Things happen in fights," I argued. "If he says something to upset you, you could—"

"Do you really think," Billy interrupted in a menacing tone, "with me knowing how he's feeling right now that *anything* he could say would make me angry enough to hurt him?" He glared at me until I looked away. "I'll go find James. Grandpa, make sure she stays here."

Grandpa nodded, and Billy walked out.

"Grandpa!" I begged, but he shook his head.

"This needs to happen, baby." He put a hand on my shoulder.

"Fine," I snapped, shaking him off. "I'll just go prepare to tend to their wounds."

With my head held high, I marched out of the room. First, I went outside and confirmed that the hose was connected to the spigot. As I walked back toward the door, I heard raised voices coming from behind the barn. Fear gnawed at my stomach. I remembered how Myron Wilcox had looked after Billy was done with him and shuddered. I wanted to believe they wouldn't hurt each other, but I just didn't know if Billy knew how to hold back in a fight.

Apparently, he did. About five minutes after I finished gathering towels, I heard someone turn on the hose. I went outside to find Billy covered in dirt with a cut on his cheek but otherwise all right. After he finished rinsing off, I tossed him a towel.

"Well?" I asked as he dried off.

"Well, what?" His tone was almost pleasant.

"Well, what happened? How did it go?"

"How it was supposed to," he said. "I'm fine. James is physically fine, and hopefully, this will help him get more emotionally fine, too."

I looked him in the eye. "You really think it will?"

He shrugged one shoulder. "The therapist does, and she went to school long enough to know." He walked toward the garden.

I went back inside to help Grandpa cook supper. The whole time, I kept peeking outside to see if James would come clean up, but he didn't. When the food was ready, I went to the back door.

"Supper's ready!" I bellowed.

Billy came toward the house.

"Go get James!" he yelled back as he approached

me. "He's in the barn."

I sighed at my own thoughtlessness – I'd forgotten James wouldn't hear me– and walked to the barn door. James was pitching hay down from the loft. He was dirty but looked unhurt. I waved my hands to get his attention. When he looked, I motioned for him to come with me. He glanced at his watch before climbing down. "Supper?" he asked.

I nodded.

"Just let me clean up a little first," he said, heading for the hose without meeting my eyes.

I walked back to the house and fixed my plate.

Grandpa, Billy, and I were all sitting at the table when James came in.

He looked straight at Billy. "I didn't mean those things I said to you."

"I know," Billy told him.

"And I shouldn't have hit you," James continued. "Although I think you wanted me to. Someone talked to Dr. Simmons, right?"

Billy and I both pointed at Grandpa.

James sighed. "I'm still sorry," he told Billy. "I—"

"James," Billy said, holding up a hand. He glanced down at himself to show he wasn't hurt. "It's fine."

James looked relieved and sat down.

Grandpa tapped him on the arm. "The frustration and anger you're feeling is normal, James. We won't take it personally if you blow up at us, OK?"

Seeing that he'd stopped talking, James nodded. "OK, Grandpa," he said in an unsure tone.

Grandpa seemed satisfied and reached for the

corn.

James looked at Billy and me with an expression that clearly meant, "I have no idea what he just said. Was it important?"

"Later," I mouthed and started eating. As I chewed, I wondered if any of us would ever be able to have a normal conversation with James again.

A few nights later, we all gathered around the TV to watch a police drama. It was one of the only shows Grandpa actually enjoyed, probably because the main character was a Marine. During one of the commercial breaks, an advertisement for an insurance company came on that included a talking lizard.

Billy looked at the creature and said, "Do you think that lizard has a tiny car that he insures with them or that he's just a paid spokesman?"

Grandpa and I laughed, but James just looked between all of us, puzzled. Not wanting him to feel left out, I reached for the dry erase board that we kept on the shelf under the coffee table.

"It's fine, Ally," James muttered.

Determined to include him, I grabbed the board anyway.

"I said it's fine!" he snapped.

Stunned, I set the board back down, unsure what I'd done wrong or why it had upset it him so much. "James, I—"

"I'm sorry, Ally," he said, running a hand through his hair.

"It's OK," I told him, though my heart was still smarting.

He gave a half-hearted nod and went to his room.

When he was gone, Grandpa laid a hand on my shoulder "Remember, he's not really upset at you, baby. He's just got so much anger inside that it sloshes over."

"I know, Grandpa," I said with a sigh. "That doesn't make it easy."

"I know," Grandpa said, giving my shoulder a comforting squeeze. "I know."

The next few weeks were really hard for me. Every time, I interacted with James, I felt as though I was walking on eggshells. He only actually snapped at me a handful of times. I always told him it was fine and not to worry about it, but I could tell he noticed how much it hurt my feelings, which only made him feel worse. Fortunately, Billy and Grandpa handled it better.

The only good thing that happened during that time was that Grandpa finally decided to get cable. I would have preferred Wi-Fi or cell phones for all of us, but it was a start. I suspected Grandpa only did it to give James something to do in the time he normally would have practiced playing his instruments; but it gave all of us more options for entertainment.

As school drew nearer, James had fewer angry outbursts but still wasn't himself. He barely spoke to us at all and just nodded when we spoke to him, whether he understood us or not. I knew he was dreading going back to school. Any time we discussed it, he intentionally ignored the conversation. I, on the other hand, was beyond ready for school to start. It would be a welcome escape from the tension at home.

Two Sundays before school started, Lee came up to me before Sunday school.

"Good morning, Ally," he said.

"Good morning," I replied, eyeing the CD case in his hand.

"I know this is short notice, but I was wondering if you would sing the special music next Sunday. It's the last Sunday before school starts, and I think it would be nice to have a student sing."

"Sure." Excitement coursed through me. "Do you have a song in mind?" I looked pointedly at the CD.

"You caught me," he said, holding it out to me. "They play this song on the radio a lot, so I figured you'd already know it. Plus, we already have the background music. Do you think you can be ready by next week?"

"Definitely."

"Thanks, Ally. I really appreciate it."

I smiled as he hurried away. I hadn't expected to have the chance to do *my thing* before school started. It was the perfect way to start the year.

Over the next few days, I practiced the song frequently in my spare time. On Wednesday night, James walked by my bedroom door while I was practicing. I stopped mid-verse as a thought occurred to me. Since James couldn't hear, maybe he wouldn't want me to sing. Dread filled my stomach. Surely, my cousin wouldn't want me to give up my thing. That would be awful.

Frowning, I turned off my CD player and went to

find James. He was in his room hanging clothes in his closet, but he paused when I came in.

"What's up?" he asked, setting his shirts on the bed.

"Do you mind if I sing on Sunday?"

When he didn't respond right away, I went to the living room and grabbed the white board. After I wrote my question on it, I went back to his room and held it up for him to see.

"No. It's fine."

"Are you sure? I mean...you can't..."

"You love singing, Ally," he said, picking up his shirts and turning back to the closet. "You shouldn't stop just because of me."

Relief coursed through me. I should've known my cousin wouldn't be that selfish.

"OK. I just wanted to check."

He didn't turn around. He'd missed that last comment, but I decided it didn't matter. His answer was clear.

On Sunday morning, I took extra time getting ready. I put on my favorite sun dress and straightened my hair, but somehow, I was still ready ten minutes before everyone else. Rolling my eyes, I sat on the couch and turned on the TV. Some things never changed.

All through Sunday school, I fidgeted and tried to ignore the butterflies in my stomach. After the church service started, I sang all of the songs, thinking of them as my warm-up exercises. Then, it was finally my turn.

"Miss Kallyna Griffin will now sing for us," Pastor

Benjamin said.

I did my best to hide my irritation as I took the stage. The pastor was the only person who ever called me by my full name.

Pushing that thought aside, I picked up the microphone and nodded to the man running the sound. I smiled at the crowd as the intro music started to play. Then, I looked at James, as I had before, and my smile faltered.

James was looking at me, desperately trying to smile, but his eyes showed the agony he felt inside. At that moment, it hit me, really hit me, that James was deaf. I'd known for months, but somehow, I'd never fully accepted it. James would never hear again. Ever. The one who'd helped me find my voice would never hear anyone's voice again as long as he lived. Tears sprang to my eyes. Mortified, I set the microphone on the pulpit and sprinted off the stage. I ran behind the church and collapsed onto my knees, tears streaming down my cheeks. *Why God?* I asked silently. *Why did You let this happen?*

After a minute, the door to the sanctuary opened and closed. I just knew it was James, coming to make everything OK, as he had at the talent show.

When I looked up, all my hopes crashed to the ground. It wasn't James. It was Grandpa.

"Where's James?" I asked, choking back tears.

He had to be coming. He had to be. James could never know I was this upset and not try to help me.

"He couldn't come, baby," Grandpa said, sitting down next to me on the floor and pulling me into his arms. "He just couldn't."

I buried my face against his shoulder and sobbed. At that moment, I knew that the James I had always depended on was gone. Grandpa rubbed my back soothingly until my tears subsided. Then he let me go.

"Why don't you go to the bathroom, wash your face and then go out to the car and wait for us?" He handed me the keys.

"Yes, sir." I did as he suggested.

As I sat in the car waiting, I had an agonizing internal debate. I loved singing for an audience. It was *my thing*. After years of searching, I'd finally found it, and nothing made me happier. But now, James couldn't hear me sing, and as much as I hated to admit it, that changed everything. By the time the church service was over, I had reached a decision. As long as James couldn't hear me, I would never sing for an audience again.

9

—THE BULLYING LESSON

School started on a Wednesday that year. On Tuesday night, I spent half an hour trying on different outfits to decide what to wear the next day. At long last, I picked out a pair of jeans and a plaid top to wear and then went out to the living room where Billy was watching TV. Figuring it was as good a way as any to pass the time, I joined him on the couch. That's when I noticed he was watching one of my favorite musicals. Billy had always claimed that musicals were stupid because people in real life didn't randomly burst into song like that. And yet, there he sat, watching one by himself.

"What's the matter with you?" I demanded.

He blinked and looked at me as if I were the one behaving strangely.

"What do you mean?"

I pointed at the TV and raised my eyebrows.

He looked over, listened to a teenager sing about hating geometry, and scowled. "Who sings about their worst subject?" he asked, reaching for the remote and turning off the TV. "How can you possibly like that kind of stuff, Ally?"

"Why don't you tell me? You were the one

watching it."

His glare could have peeled paint. "I was *not* watching that. I was thinking, and it just happened to be on."

I studied him suspiciously. Of our entire family, I would have picked Billy as the least likely to become a philosopher. He wasn't given to sitting and thinking.

"Something on your mind, Billy?"

"I'm worried about school tomorrow."

I would've thought he was joking, except I read the truth in his eyes. "Why?" I asked, trying to hide my surprise. "You've always done OK in school, and you have a lot of friends."

"I'm not worried about me," he said, shaking his head as if the idea was ludicrous. "I'm worried about James."

I sighed deeply. James had barely said a word to any of us since church on Sunday, and he'd only nibbled at his supper that night.

"Me, too," I admitted.

"I don't know how they expect him to keep up in his classes," Billy said. "Letting him sit at the front and having someone give him notes won't be enough."

I nodded. We had both decided those things were inadequate when Grandpa told us about them weeks before, but that wasn't my main concern. "I'm more worried about people picking on him."

Billy clenched his fists. "They wouldn't dare."

I rolled my eyes. "Teenagers can be cruel, Billy. Just because he can't help being deaf doesn't mean—"

"They wouldn't dare," Billy interrupted, "because

they know I'll beat them to a pulp if they do. And if they don't know that, they'll find out really quick."

I considered that for a second. The fact that guys hesitated to even borrow a pencil from me testified to just how effective a deterrent Billy could be. But still…

"You can't be everywhere, Billy. And you know James won't tell you if anyone bothers him."

Billy frowned. "I know, but between the two of us, I think we can keep an eye on him." He gazed pointedly at me. "And *you* better tell me if you notice anyone messing with him."

"Of course, I will!" I told him indignantly.

He nodded, satisfied, and then smiled teasingly. "So, did you finally decide what you're wearing tomorrow?"

I narrowed my eyes. "As a matter of fact—"

I was cut off by James running out of his room, down the hall, and into the bathroom. He slammed the door behind him, and after a second, we heard the unmistakable sound of retching.

We'd all eaten the same thing, and the rest of us were fine. James hadn't gone anywhere to catch a virus, which left only one explanation. "I guess James is worried about tomorrow, too."

Billy nodded and turned the TV back on. He didn't say anything but pretended he hadn't noticed James's flight to the bathroom.

Lord, please help James calm down, I prayed before snatching the remote out of Billy's hand.

That night, I had trouble falling asleep. When I finally did, I dreamed that I had to sit next to Jenny in all of my classes. A bad omen if there ever was one.

The next morning, all three of us got ready for school quickly. James looked pale during breakfast, but he ate it without throwing up, which I thought was a good sign. When we were ready to leave, we assembled in the kitchen, so Grandpa could give us our lunch money checks, as always.

"I hope you have a good day," Grandpa said, passing out the checks. "And if any of you need anything, you can call me. I'll be here." He looked at James as he said the last part.

James nodded, although I wasn't sure he'd understood him. Lately, James had been nodding so much he could have been mistaken for a bobble head. We'd all learned that it meant he didn't want us to repeat what we'd said rather than actually confirming his comprehension.

Grandpa hesitated. I could tell he wanted to say more on that subject, but apparently, he thought better of it. Instead, he opened the door and told us not to be late as we walked out to Billy's car. One of the perks of Billy being a senior was that he could drive us all to school. Of course, we'd have to ride the bus home during football season, but that was a lot better than riding it both ways.

"You take the front, Ally," James said, climbing into the backseat.

I frowned. I knew James just wanted to make it easier to cut himself off from any attempt at conversation on the way there, but following him into the backseat and badgering him seemed like a bad idea.

Billy drove us to school in silence. I wanted to turn on the radio, but I didn't want James to feel left out. As I stared out the window, I decided that I should join a club or sports team this year. Anything to give me more time away from home and all this stress.

When we made it to school, I practically jumped out of the car and raced for the building. Suddenly, I just couldn't take it anymore. I was ready to see Missy and just have things go back to normal. Halfway there, I felt a pang of guilt as I realized that for James, there was no back to normal. There was nowhere he could go that would make things feel like they had before. Feeling ashamed, I glanced back.

James and Billy were walking...well, more like trudging...to the building together.

After a moment's pause, I decided that Billy being with him was enough and continued my race for the school.

I went straight to the gym where we always waited until the bell rang. Anxiously, I scanned the crowd and sighed with relief when I saw Missy sitting in the bleachers and waving to get my attention. I walked over and sat with her, throwing my practically empty backpack onto the bleachers beside me.

"Where are James and Billy?" She looked toward the door.

"They were walking slower than I wanted to," I said in what I hoped was a nonchalant tone. "Why?"

She shrugged. "I just figured you'd walk in with them. How was the rest of your summer?" It had been several weeks since I'd been to her house.

"Fine," I said. "How was yours?"

"OK. I spent most of it finishing the summer reading."

"What books did you—?"

"Hi, Ally. Hi, Missy," a voice from behind me interrupted. "How was your summer?"

Missy frowned slightly, but even without that hint, I recognized the voice I loathed so much.

"All right. How was yours, Jenny?" I asked, turning to face her.

"Great," she said. "Tony Rawlings and I started going out, and he is *such* a wonderful boyfriend."

I gritted my teeth but forced my expression to remain at least semi-pleasant. Tony was a very attractive junior who played on the football team. Of the girls at school not pining after Billy, at least half of them had a crush on Tony. And he and Jenny were dating. Of course, they were.

"That's great, Jenny," Missy said. "I'm glad you're happy." She actually sounded sincere, which made her either a very good actress or a very good Christian. Possibly both.

"Thanks," Jenny said. "Did either of you find a boyfriend?"

We hadn't, and she knew it. Between Billy's threats and Missy's shyness, we'd be lucky if a boy ever spoke to us.

I bit back an angry retort, not wanting to give her the satisfaction of knowing she'd upset me. "No, we were busy," I said.

It wasn't a lie. I was very busy doing…stuff.

"Oh, yeah, I heard you sang at your church," she said pleasantly. "I mean you almost sang. It kind of reminds you of the talent show, doesn't it?"

I felt like I'd been punched in the stomach. For a moment, I was kneeling behind the church, sobbing, hoping that James would come. Triumph glowed in Jenny eyes, and I was seriously wondering if punching her in the face would be worth getting suspended when Missy came to my rescue.

"Well, Ally won second place in the talent show," she said. "I'm sure something good will happen this time, too."

Jenny's smile faltered for a second, but she hitched it back in place. "I'm sure," she said, looking at Missy. "Did you have time to finish the summer reading? You would have had to read a whole book each month."

Missy looked down self-consciously.

"We both did," I jumped in. "That's what we were talking about when you joined us."

Jenny looked back at me. "I guess that would be what you'd talk about if it was the most exciting thing you did this summer," she said with a smirk.

Then she started to walk away. I was halfway through a sigh of relief when she turned back. "Did you know the band's going to Florida this spring?" she asked. "James probably told you. I'm sure he *heard* all about it." She paused for dramatic effect. "Oh, no. I guess, he didn't, did he?"

My fists clenched involuntarily, and I took a step toward her. Missy grabbed hold of my arm to hold me back just as the bell rang.

Jenny sauntered off to join the throng of students heading for the main part of the school building, and I took a deep breath.

"Hitting her isn't worth getting suspended," Missy told me. She let go of my arm now that there was no one left for me to attack.

"That's an opinion," I told her and headed for my locker.

I was still fuming when I got to my first period class. How dare Jenny make fun of James? But my anger quickly gave way to sorrow. James would be very disappointed that he couldn't go to Florida with the band. If only they'd gone last year instead. I was so deep in thought that I didn't notice that someone had sat down next to me until he said, "Hi, I'm Eli."

I turned and looked into a pair of gorgeous, dark eyes. Startled, I studied the boy for a second before I answered. He had short black hair, broad shoulders, and appeared to be of Native American descent.

"I'm Ally," I said, hoping I hadn't been gazing at him for too long. "Are you new?"

He was. I was absolutely positive. There was no way under heaven I could have gone to the same school as this boy last year and not noticed.

"Yeah," he said. "We moved here over the summer because of my dad's job."

"Cool," I said, trying to keep the question out of my voice. I wouldn't have been very happy having to start over at a new high school as a sophomore, but he might have felt differently. "Do you like it so far?"

He shrugged. "It was kind of lonesome this summer, but I'm hoping to make some friends now that school's started."

"School's a good place to make friends," I said and cringed inwardly. He'd basically just said that, hadn't he?

He smiled, so I guess he didn't think I sounded too stupid.

"It sure is," he said as the teacher walked to the front of the class.

"Nice to meet you, Eli. Let me know if you need help finding anything."

There. Two full sentences. A new record.

"Thanks, Ally. I'll do that," he said.

Then the teacher, a large gray-haired man with glasses, introduced himself as Mr. Thompson, and the class officially began.

Meeting Eli was the highlight of my entire day. I'm not sure if that indicates how much I liked him or how boring the rest of the day was. None of my classes seemed interesting at all, not even English, my favorite subject. On the bright side, I had no classes with Jenny. On the dim side, I didn't have any with Missy either.

Our high school was small enough that all of the students ate lunch at the same time, so at least I wasn't stuck by myself there. Missy and I met each other outside of the cafeteria before we got in the lunch line. While we waited, I told her all about Eli and my conversation with him during first period. She, in turn, told me about her day, which unfortunately included two classes with Jenny. By the time we got our food, there were only a few tables left in the cafeteria, so we quickly picked one and sat down.

"Since you're not doing ballet, will you join a club or team this year?" Missy asked.

I took a swig of my milk. "Yeah, I think I will. Could I borrow your phone, so I can look through the list?"

"Sure," she said, fishing it out of her backpack and handing it to me.

I pulled up the list on the school website and scrolled through it, pausing when I got to cross country. Last year, I'd passed it over because it offered little opportunity for applause. This year, though, I was looking for escape, and running until I was too tired to think sounded great.

"I think I'll join the cross-country team," I said, handing the phone back to Missy. "I'll sign up after school and see when practice starts."

Missy nodded and kept eating. If she thought my decision was out of character, she kept it to herself. After a minute, she said, "There's James. Do you think he'd want to sit with us?"

I followed her gaze and saw my cousin looking a little lost as he wandered around with his lunch tray.

"Good idea," I told Missy and waved him over.

When James saw me, he quickly walked over to join us, looking relieved. As he sank onto the seat next to me, I turned my face deliberately toward him.

"How's it going?" I asked.

"All right," he said, though his eyes said different. "What about you?"

"Pretty boring," I said. "I hope my classes get more interesting than they were today."

He nodded, and I could have kicked myself. That sentence was way too complex for him speech read.

"Hi, James," Missy said. She waved as she said it, which got his attention.

"What?" he asked her.

"Hi, James," she repeated, waving again.

"Hi, Missy," he said. "How's your day going?"

She shrugged. "So-so." She held her hand out flat with her fingers apart and rocked it back and forth to help get her point across.

James nodded.

"There seems to be a lot of that going around," he said, then silently blessed his food and started eating.

I smiled at Missy, grateful that she'd taken the time to communicate with James, before turning my attention to my lunch.

After a minute, Billy walked into the cafeteria. He was with a group of his football friends, but he scanned the crowded room. I stared at him until he caught sight of us. When he met my gaze, he glanced at James and raised his eyebrows, his question as clear as day. Is he OK?

I nodded to let him know that he was as good as could be expected.

Billy jerked his head slightly in acknowledgement and turned back to his friends.

I looked at James, hoping he hadn't noticed our silent exchange.

He was gazing at me with an almost amused

expression on his face.

"What?" I demanded, trying to play dumb.

"I'm deaf, Ally. Not blind."

Missy giggled as he started eating again.

I glared at her in mock annoyance and then went back to the reddish-brown concoction on my plate that was supposed to be spaghetti.

The rest of the day passed slowly. After my last class ended, I stopped by the gym and signed up for cross-country. One of the P.E. teachers told me that practice started the next day after school. I thanked him and headed for the parking lot to meet my cousins.

"So, how was your first day?" Billy asked after we got in the car, looking at both of us. I knew he meant the question more for James, but when James didn't answer, I decided someone needed to.

"All right. Kind of boring."

"Yeah, sophomore year wasn't my favorite," Billy said sympathetically. "Do you have Mrs. Polk for English?"

When I nodded, he patted my shoulder.

"It's just a year," he said. "You'll make it." Then he looked at James. "How was your day?"

James wouldn't meet his eyes. "OK, I guess. Can we go home now?"

There was a hint of desperation in his voice. Billy looked concerned, but he cranked the car without another word.

When we got home, James dropped his backpack on the porch. "I'm going for a walk," he muttered before practically sprinting for the field behind the garden.

Billy and I exchanged a worried look.

Grandpa chose that moment to come out of the house. He looked at our faces and James's discarded backpack. "I'm guessing this means it didn't go well," he said, a question in his voice.

"We don't know how it went," Billy said. "James said it was OK, but he'd probably say that if he was dying."

"Billy—" Grandpa began in a mollifying tone, but Billy cut him off.

"I'm serious, Grandpa. How are we supposed to help him if he won't tell us anything? Most of the time he won't even tell us when he doesn't understand what we say!" He was close to shouting by the end of this statement.

"I know it's hard," Grandpa said, looking at both of us. "Eventually James will figure out that he can't deal with this on his own. Until then, we just have to be patient."

Billy ran his fingers through his hair agitatedly.

"He's not ready to be at school," I said, crossing my arms.

Grandpa sighed. "I know, but there really isn't anything we can do about it."

"You could homeschool him," I said with sudden inspiration.

Grandpa shook his head. "I couldn't begin to teach him eleventh-grade material, and even if I could, I wouldn't. James needs to learn how to live his life now that he's deaf, and hiding on this farm is not the way to do it."

I suppressed a scream of frustration. When would this get easier?

Grandpa squeezed my shoulder. "It'll be OK, baby. God will get James through this, and He'll get us through it, too."

I clung to Grandpa's words, wanting desperately to believe them.

After a moment, Grandpa let me go. "So how was your first day?" he asked, looking between Billy and me.

"Normal," Billy said with a shrug.

"Pretty good," I said. "I joined the cross-country team."

Grandpa smiled. "That's great, baby."

"They practice at the same time as the football team, so you can ride home with me after practice," Billy told me.

"That works out well," I said and then frowned. "But what about James? With him not doing band—"

"He'll ride home on the bus," Grandpa said, "just as you would have if you hadn't joined a team." He looked between the two of us. "Do you have any homework?"

We shook our heads.

"Then you have the afternoon free."

We both smiled half-heartedly and headed into the house.

James didn't come back from his walk until suppertime. He was quiet while we ate and throughout the rest of the evening. When we prayed together as a family that night, his prayer lasted about ten seconds, and he went straight to bed after Grandpa said amen. We all watched him go.

Grandpa bowed his head again. "Lord, please be with James. Help him deal with all the changes in his life, and show us how to be there for him. Amen."

"Amen," Billy and I echoed and headed for bed.

The second day of school passed much like the first, minus the morning confrontation with Jenny. Eli spoke to me in first period again, much to my delight. He just asked me where the library was, but I still considered it progress. I met Missy again for lunch.

After we got our food and sat down, she pulled a flyer out of her backpack. "Did you see this?" she asked, holding it out to me.

I stopped scanning the cafeteria for James and looked at the paper. It announced that the Becoming Better Buzzards Club would be holding a talent show and needed volunteers to perform. The audience would have to pay for admission, and the proceeds would benefit a local homeless shelter.

"Are you going to enter?" Missy asked.

For half a second, I considered it. Then I remembered James's face the last time I tried to sing. "No," I said. "Now put that away. I don't want James to see it if he comes to sit with us."

Missy frowned but did as I asked. I couldn't blame her for feeling confused. The last time we'd talked about singing, I'd told her I loved it and wanted to do it as often as I could. She couldn't possibly know that *my thing* had been lost with James's hearing, but I wasn't feeling up to telling her. At least not yet.

James didn't sit with Missy and me at lunch. I kept an eye out for him in the cafeteria, but he was nowhere to be found.

Billy caught my eye again when he came in with his friends. When I shrugged helplessly, he frowned, glanced around the cafeteria, and left, presumably to find James. He came back a few minutes later and walked over to me. "He's sitting at a picnic table by himself," Billy said, quiet enough that no one at the nearby tables would hear. "He says he's fine."

I studied his face. "Do you believe him?"

"Not really," Billy said with a shrug. "But he turned down my offer to sit with him. Short of dragging him into the cafeteria, I don't see what else I can do." He sighed. "I'm going to get food. See you later."

As he walked back to stand with his friends, I wondered if James would be more receptive to Missy and me joining him than he'd been to Billy. After all, wherever my oldest cousin went, half the football team and cheerleading squad followed.

"Do you want to go sit with James?" Missy asked, reading my mind.

I bit my lip, considering. "No. If he wanted to sit with us, he would have. It's probably best to give him some space."

Missy nodded and went back to eating. I did the same, hoping that I'd made the right decision.

At the end of the day, I went to my first cross-country practice and enjoyed it thoroughly. The other runners were very welcoming, and as I'd predicted, running proved to be a good way to distract myself from everything going on in my life.

Friday came and went in the blink of an eye. As I rode home with Billy after practice, I found myself for the first time feeling sorry that it was the weekend. Two whole days of being stuck at home worrying about James. I wasn't looking forward to it.

As it turned out, I didn't have to worry about him much. James stayed shut in his room or went on walks by himself pretty much the entire weekend, except for meals and church. Something was clearly bothering him, but when we asked, he refused to talk about it. I knew it wasn't healthy for James to isolate himself like that, but it did make the weekend a lot less stressful. I would take what I could get.

I was still relieved to go back to school on Monday. The day was normal until the end when I met Billy at the gym after practice. We walked to his car together...where we found James leaning against the back door reading his American history textbook.

Billy and I shared a perplexed look.

"This can't be good," I told him.

"Nope," he said, seeming to brace himself. "What are you doing here?" Billy asked when we were still several feet away.

James kept reading as if he hadn't heard him...which of course he hadn't.

Billy walked over and tapped James's book. "What are you doing here?" he asked as soon as James looked up.

James shrugged. "I figured I'd wait and ride home with you."

Billy stared at him incredulously. "You figured you'd wait almost two hours in one-hundred-degree heat to ride home with us?"

James shrugged again and tried to get in the car. It was still locked. He stared at the door for a while and then turned back around to look at us.

No one said anything for at least five seconds.

"Are you really going to make me ask?" Billy said.

When James didn't respond, Billy nodded.

"Fine. Why don't you want to ride the bus?" He pointed at a school bus on the other side of the parking lot.

"Why would I ride the bus now that you've got a car?" James asked.

The answer to that question couldn't have been more obvious if it had been spray painted on the side of the gym in neon orange.

Billy narrowed his eyes.

"Tell me what's going on," he demanded. "Or am I going to have to figure it out myself?"

James sighed. "Can we go home now?"

Billy rolled his eyes and unlocked the car. "Figure it out myself, it is," he muttered, heading for the driver's side.

I slid into the passenger seat, wondering who or what James could possibly want to avoid that badly.

It was two weeks before we found out. During that time, Eli and I went from just classmates to friendly acquaintances, and I avoided Jenny like the plague. A few of my cross-country teammates who remembered my performance in the talent show the previous year also tried to persuade me to sing in the upcoming one, but I steadfastly refused. It didn't matter if it was for a good cause or that it was *my thing*. If James couldn't hear me, I wasn't singing, and that was that.

One Monday, my fourth period teacher let us out a little late. I was rushing to the cafeteria, hoping the line wouldn't be too long yet, when I heard Austin's unmistakable voice.

"How's it feel to be deaf and *dumb*?"

I froze and looked over, dreading what I'd see. James was sitting at a picnic table alone, trying to eat his lunch. Austin was standing across from him, looking down at him with a mocking expression. Several of his friends were standing behind him, laughing.

Fury bubbled up inside me. I took two steps in their direction, ready to do whatever it took to make Austin stop, when I remembered what Billy said during Disciple Youth weekend a few months ago.

Next time, come get me.

Heart pounding, I spun around and headed toward the hallway that led to the cafeteria.

In less than a minute, I found my oldest cousin walking at a leisurely pace and chatting with a cheerleader I'd never met. He was laughing at something she'd said, but when I walked up, the smile melted off his face.

"Are you OK?" he asked.

I nodded, slightly out of breath. "I'm fine, but James isn't. Austin has him cornered by the picnic tables, and—"

"He what?" Billy asked, a mixture of disbelief and anger in his voice.

"He's taunting him in front of a group and—"

Billy stepped past me and strode down the hall, his face a thundercloud. I tried to keep up with him but fell behind. His legs were a lot longer than mine. I made it outside to the picnic tables just as Billy finished forcing his way through the crowd. I barely had the chance to hear two words Austin was saying before Billy interrupted him.

"What do you think you're doing?" he asked.

The crowd grew quiet at Billy's tone, and I gritted my teeth in frustration. I wanted to see what was going on, but there was a crowd of people between my cousins and me. I considered shoving my way through like Billy and then thought of a better way. Quickly, I climbed onto a picnic table and looked over everyone's heads.

James was still sitting at a picnic table with his lunch, his eyes downcast.

Austin was standing across the table from him, facing Billy.

"I was just talking to James," Austin said. "I wanted to find out what it's like to be deaf and *dumb*."

Billy clenched his fists. "How dare you bother him? He's deaf. It's not as if he has any control over it."

Austin shrugged, a cruel expression on his face.

"Why shouldn't I? Your cousin's always been a freak. Now he's just more of one."

My stomach clenched in disgust. How could I have ever had a crush on this guy?

Billy stepped closer to Austin. "Leave him alone."

Austin looked into Billy's eyes, enjoying the crowd too much to heed the warning flashing there.

"Or what?"

For a moment, neither of them moved. I could tell by Austin's smirk that he didn't think Billy would hit him. He obviously didn't know my oldest cousin as well as he thought.

Billy glanced at James. He would back down if James wanted him to, but James didn't even look up. He just kept staring at his plate, his expression tormented.

Billy turned back to Austin, his eyes filled with unchecked rage. He hit Austin with a right hook that knocked him onto the picnic table seat. Austin stood up and took a swing, but Billy dodged it and tackled him to the ground.

The students in the crowd had started chanting "Fight! Fight! Fight!"

I almost joined them. I knew Grandpa didn't approve of Billy solving problems with his fists, but these were extenuating circumstances.

Billy and Austin rolled around for a few seconds, but Billy ended up on top. He punched Austin across the face a couple times and then pulled him up by his shirt. Austin stared up at him, his eyes wide in fear.

"If you *ever* bother James again," Billy told him,

"this will seem like a cake walk." He let go of his shirt and stood up. "That goes for all of you," he said, glaring at the assembled crowd.

None of them met his gaze.

"What is going on here?" a teacher demanded, running up.

I rolled my eyes. Now the adult supervision showed up.

"Austin needed a lesson on bullying," Billy told her, his tone matter-of-fact. "There were no teachers around, so I taught him myself."

She stared at him, completely dumbfounded. After an awkward pause, she found her voice. "Go to the principal's office."

"Yes, ma'am," Billy said and walked in that direction.

"The rest of you, go eat lunch." She trailed after Billy.

When the other students had all cleared out, I tapped James on the shoulder.

He looked up at me with anguished eyes.

"Are you OK?" I asked even though I already knew the answer.

"I want to go home," he said.

"Then go home," someone behind me said.

I jumped and turned around. Missy was standing a couple steps away. I hadn't realized she was out here, too.

"Go home," she said again, making sure James could see her clearly. Then she looked at me. "Your grandpa will have to come to the school to talk to the principal anyway. Why don't you all go home?"

I smiled at her. "Good idea. Let's go, James."

"What?" he asked.

I started to just motion for him to follow me, but Missy sat down across from him, took out a pen and paper, and wrote down everything she'd just said. When she was finished, she handed it to James, who read it and nodded.

"Thank you," he told her sincerely as he stood up. I couldn't tell if he meant for the suggestion or for taking the time to write it down.

"You're welcome," she said.

Their gazes met for a moment. Then James turned and walked into the building.

"I'll see you tomorrow," I told Missy, following him inside.

When we got to the office, Mrs. MacDougall told us that Grandpa was already on his way to the school, so James and I sat down and waited. After a few minutes, Billy came out of Mr. Demmings's office and joined us.

"What's the verdict?" I twirled a strand of hair around my finger.

"One-week suspension."

"How long?" James asked.

"One week," Billy repeated slowly.

James nodded. "I'm sorry."

"For what?" Billy asked.

James looked at the floor and didn't answer.

Billy tapped him on the shoulder, and James looked up. "Answer me. What are you sorry for?"

James shrugged, but Billy wouldn't let it go.

"What are you sorry for?" he repeated. He wasn't angry, just insistent.

Mr. Demmings opened the door to his office, but he didn't intervene.

Mrs. MacDougall was watching them intently as well.

James still didn't answer.

"For being deaf?" Billy asked. "For Austin deciding that's a good reason to mess with you? What?"

I'm not sure how much of that James understood, but he wouldn't meet Billy's eyes. "I don't know."

Billy tapped him again. "Yes, you do," he said, "but you're wrong. None of this is your fault."

James's shoulders sagged. It was obvious he still felt responsible for everything that had happened.

I met Billy's gaze and saw only frustration. His words hadn't reached James.

I squared my shoulders. Billy had tried. Now it was my turn. I turned to look at Mrs. MacDougall. "Do you have a notepad and pen I can borrow?"

She handed them to me. I thanked her and then wrote, *none of this is your fault.* When I finished, I held it out to James.

He read it and nodded. "I know," he muttered.

I shook my head and started writing again.

"You have nothing to be sorry for," I said, pointing at the notepad where I'd written the same thing.

James sighed deeply as he read it. "I know," he

said, meeting my eyes this time.

We held each other's gaze for several long seconds.

"Then, stop apologizing," I said. I was about to write that too, but James held up his hand. "I understood you." He paused before adding, "And I'll try."

I looked James in the face for another long moment and then nodded. It was hard to be sure, but I thought I'd really gotten through to him. I handed the notepad and pen back to Mrs. MacDougall and thanked her again.

Billy smiled and gave me an approving nod. We both knew that James needed to stop feeling responsible for everything that had changed as a result of his hearing loss.

We sat quietly for a while. I was getting my emotions under control, and I suspected Billy and James were too, although they did everything in their power to keep from showing it.

Then Billy broke the silence. "Austin's bothered you before, hasn't he?"

I tapped James and nodded toward Billy, who repeated his question. James frowned, clearly not understanding.

Mrs. MacDougall wordlessly held out the notepad.

Billy took it and wrote down his question.

James read it and nodded.

Billy clenched his fists as a thought occurred to me.

"Is that why you won't ride the bus?" I asked.

"What?" James said.

Billy handed me the notepad, and I jotted down what I'd said.

James read it and then nodded.

Billy snatched the notepad from me and wrote his next question, bearing down so hard that he almost ripped the paper. "Austin's been bothering you since the second day of school?" Billy demanded. "Why didn't you tell me?"

"He's your friend," James said after he read it. "You enjoy hanging out with him. I didn't want to mess that up."

Billy rolled his eyes. "I don't want to be friends with anyone who treats my family like that," he growled.

James understood his meaning if not his words, and we both smiled.

"Good riddance," I said, and Billy chuckled.

"I really hope you aren't laughing about your suspension," Grandpa said, walking into the office.

Mr. Demmings walked out of his door the instant Grandpa spoke. "He wasn't." He shook Grandpa's hand. "Come into my office, Mr. Griffin. Billy, you come too." He looked at us thoughtfully. "Actually, why don't all of you come?"

Billy got up and followed them into the office. Confused, I turned to James.

"He wants us to go, too," I told him, nodding my head toward the office.

He raised his eyebrows but stood, and we walked into Mr. Demmings's office together. I couldn't help but feel nervous. I didn't think I was in trouble, but it was still the principal's office. Nothing good had ever come from being called to the principal's office.

When we entered, Mr. Demmings was already settled behind his large, oak desk, and Billy and Grandpa were seated across from him. There were two more chairs next to them, so James and I sat down.

Mr. Demmings surveyed the three of us. "From what I heard out there," he said at last. "Austin Peterson has been bullying James, and the fight put a stop to it. Is that right?" He looked at all of us.

"Yes sir, it is," Billy answered.

Mr. Demmings eyed him, puzzled. "Why didn't you tell me that before?"

"You didn't ask," Billy said with a shrug. "The school's zero tolerance policy is pretty clear. There's no excuse for fighting. I didn't figure my reason mattered all that much."

Mr. Demmings drummed his fingers on the desk. "In terms of punishment, it may not, but it helps me understand the situation better." He turned his gaze to James. "If Austin's been bothering you, why didn't you tell a teacher rather than asking Billy to handle it?"

James glanced at me, silently asking what he'd said.

Instead of telling him, I took a deep breath and looked Mr. Demmings in the eye. "James didn't ask Billy to handle it. I did."

He frowned. "Why? Don't you think telling a teacher would've been a better option?"

I studied my hands, unsure how to tell him why it

was definitely not a better option.

"Of course not." Billy came to my rescue. "What would a teacher do?"

"A teacher would have stopped him without using violence. That is always a better option," Mr. Demmings said, his voice ringing with conviction.

Billy met his gaze unwaveringly. "With all due respect, Mr. Demmings, that's not true in this case. You don't know Austin like I do. A teacher might've stopped him this time. They might've even given him detention or something, but that wouldn't bother him enough to make him stop. He would've messed with James again. That's just the way he is. That's why I had to put a stop to it. Now, Austin won't dare to so much as look at James funny, and neither will anyone else because they know what'll happen if they do."

Mr. Demmings considered that for a second. "Do you agree with him, Ally?" he asked, raising his eyebrows. I could tell by his expression that he already knew my opinion and wanted to see if I had the guts to tell him.

"Yes, sir," I said hesitantly. "That's why I got him."

Mr. Demmings looked at James. "And what do you think?"

James looked at him uncertainly. "Could you repeat the question?"

"What do you,"—he pointed at James—"think?" He touched his finger to his temple.

"About the fight?" James asked.

Mr. Demmings nodded.

James turned and gazed thoughtfully at Billy for a moment and then looked right at Mr. Demmings. "I think it was inevitable. Billy's never put up with anyone messing with me or Ally, and I didn't really expect him to start now. He was bound to beat somebody up over it eventually, so if it had to be someone, I'm glad it was Austin because he's the one who's bothered me the most. I am sorry that it happened at school, though, because that means Billy has to be suspended, and I don't think he deserves that."

Mr. Demmings furrowed his brow. "I understand your point, but I still can't condone—"

"It's OK, Mr. Demmings," Billy said. "I know you still have to suspend me. I knew that before I ever hit Austin."

"So, you did consider the consequences?" Mr. Demmings asked, eyebrows raised.

"Of course," Billy said. "I just knew it was worth it."

Mr. Demmings studied us. "All of you seem to be under the impression that the only way to be sure Austin would stop bullying James was for Billy to handle it." He shook his head. "I want to assure you that that's not the case. I take bullying very seriously. Austin would have received much more than detention. I would have suspended him from the bus and the football team. If that didn't work, he would have been suspended from school."

Billy raised his eyebrows, clearly surprised.

My mouth dropped open in shock. It had never

occurred to me that the school would take such drastic measures.

"Now, I have to punish both you and Austin for the fight before I can even try to deal with the bullying," Mr. Demmings continued, looking at Billy. "Don't you think it would have been better to at least *try* letting the staff handle the situation first?"

Billy frowned as if he wasn't sure what to think.

I looked down at my lap. I'd gone to get Billy because he'd told me to, but I could just as easily have told a teacher. Maybe that really would have been the better option.

"That's something for you to consider next time," Mr. Demmings said. "You can all go now. Mr. Griffin, be sure to sign that you are taking James and Ally, too."

With that, we left the principal's office.

Billy drove his car home, but James and I rode with Grandpa. No one said a word the whole time. I cast furtive glances at Grandpa every so often, but I couldn't read his expression. When we got home, I filed into the living room after Billy and James sat down, waiting for the ax to fall.

Grandpa followed us in. He surveyed each of us long and hard before he finally spoke.

"Billy, I know why you fought Austin," he said each word slowly. "And Ally, I understand why you told Billy instead of a teacher. I want you both to know that I agree with Mr. Demmings. You should have reported it and let the school staff handle it. If they couldn't, then you should have come to me, and I would have dealt with the situation." He heaved a sigh. "Billy, you have to learn that you can't handle all of your problems with your fists."

Billy nodded, his eyes downcast.

"And Ally, you need to learn to trust authority figures with problems rather than your cousins."

"Yes, sir," I said, feeling the size of a flea.

"I won't be punishing either of you," Grandpa said, his expression softening. "You both made mistakes, but I can't fault your intentions. And though your methods were…unwise, they were also effective."

Grandpa turned his piercing gaze to James. "I think my only question is for you. If Austin has been bullying you, why didn't you tell me or a teacher?"

James held his gaze for several seconds before realizing he was supposed to respond. He glanced at us, his eyes a bit panicked, and swallowed hard.

"Honestly, Grandpa," James said, "I have no idea what you just said."

A look of surprise crossed Grandpa's face. Then he turned and walked into James and Billy's room.

I grinned and peeked at Billy, who was smiling too. James almost never admitted to not understanding something and never this bluntly, especially with Grandpa. Before I could contemplate James's simple statement any further, Grandpa came back with the dry erase board and marker. He quickly wrote "Why didn't you tell someone?" and handed it to James.

"About Austin?" James clarified. When Grandpa nodded, he shrugged. "Because I was trying to avoid this." He motioned to all of us sitting on the couch. "I was afraid if I told a teacher, Austin would find out, and things would get worse. And I knew if either of them"—he inclined his head toward Billy and me– "found out that Billy would pound Austin into the ground." He turned to look at Billy with a lopsided smile. "You actually held back quite a bit. I was impressed."

Billy chuckled. "I didn't want him to go to the hospital. I figured I'd get more days for that."

James gave him a blank look, so Billy reached for the dry erase board. Grandpa cleared his throat, and Billy let his hand fall into his lap.

"Later," he told James, jerking his head toward Grandpa.

"I understand, James," Grandpa said, "but there's no reason for you to put up with bullying."

"What?" James asked.

Grandpa wrote on the dry erase board and held it up. "Don't do that again."

"I won't, Grandpa," James said.

"All right, then," Grandpa said with finality. "I'm glad we had this talk. Now go do your homework or chores or something." He shooed us away with his hands.

I headed for my room, barely believing none of us was getting punished. To be fair, Billy was still suspended, but other than that, nothing. And James was talking again. He'd even smiled a couple times. As I opened my math book, I held out hope that maybe, just maybe, he'd keep doing that.

Grandpa drove James and me to and from school

while Billy was suspended. We didn't figure anything would happen on the bus, but there was no sense tempting fate. During that week and the ones that followed, I noticed a subtle change in James.

He sat with Missy and me pretty often during lunch and even sat with some of his band friends a couple times. He asked all of us to repeat things more often and only occasionally reverted back to the nod and shrug routine he had perfected over the summer. Between that and my daily conversations with Eli, sophomore year definitely took a turn for the better.

10

—WHO KNEW?

One Friday night several weeks after school started, the Becoming Better Buzzards Club held their talent show. Because it was benefitting the homeless shelter, Grandpa offered to pay for our admission. I didn't want to go, but if I didn't, I would have to explain why, which I wanted to do even less. That's how I ended up riding in the backseat as Billy drove all three of us to the school.

As soon as we entered the auditorium, Billy ditched James and me to go sit with a cheerleader.

I was about to suggest that we sit near the back when Missy waved at us from the third row. Since there was no polite way to ignore her, I walked up and sat next to my best friend. James sank into the seat beside me, looking uncomfortable. I wasn't sure why he'd decided to come when he wouldn't be able to hear any of the acts, but I'd decided not to ask.

The contestants had a lot more talent than most of those I'd competed against the previous year. I managed to enjoy several of the acts, including a hip-hop dance and a funny ventriloquist. Several of the contestants sang, and I tried not to be too jealous as I watched them. Just because I couldn't sing anymore didn't mean I should begrudge it to everyone else. Still, when one girl got a standing ovation, I was eaten alive with envy. I wanted more than anything to be in her place, filled with the excitement of pleasing the crowd. *Why, God? Why did You even let me find my thing if You were just going to take it away so soon? It's not fair.*

I glanced at James, who was clapping for a performance he couldn't hear, and guilt stabbed my heart. At least I could still hear music. He didn't even have that.

After all twenty contestants had performed, the judges took five minutes to deliberate who would win.

During the break, James turned and looked at me. "Why didn't you perform, Ally?"

I shrugged and didn't meet his gaze. "I just didn't want to."

He gave me a strange look.

"I said I just—"

"I understood you," he said. "But why not? You love to sing."

I shrugged again, unsure how to respond. I couldn't tell him the real reason, but he'd know if I lied. Fortunately, the head judge walked on stage at that moment to announce the winner. I turned to look at the stage, pretending I was eager to know who won.

James started to say something and then apparently decided not to.

I sighed in relief, hoping he would forget he'd ever asked that question by the time we got home. Whether he forgot or just decided not to ask, James never broached the subject again. Either way I was relieved.

I was in a foul mood for the rest of the weekend. It wasn't until Monday that I finally shook it off. Our school was on a nine-weeks grading system, which meant we received our first progress reports in September, four and half weeks after school started. That Monday, they cut our last class ten minutes short so that we could go back to our homerooms and get our progress reports. I smiled when Mr. Thompson handed me mine. It was all A's and B's just as I expected.

"Does that smile mean you did well?" Eli asked.

I nodded. "I thought I'd been doing fine, but it's always good to know for sure."

"Yeah, it is," he said.

I glanced at his desk, but his progress report was face down.

"How'd you do?" I asked.

"Fine," he said.

I narrowed my eyes and tried to snatch his progress report, but he beat me to it.

"You could've just asked to see it," he said, holding it up for my inspection.

"Where's the fun in that?" I asked and then looked at his grades. He had A's in all of his classes. Apparently, Eli was cute, funny, and smart. There were no down sides to this guy.

"Fine?" I said. "That's a little more than fine."

He shrugged but didn't look as though he wanted to discuss it anymore, so I let the subject drop.

"So, you're officially halfway through one grading period," I said instead. "What do you think of Mayville

High?"

He grinned, and my heart did a flip-flop.

"It's growing on me," he said as the bell rang. "See you later, Ally," he called over his shoulder, walking toward the door.

Once he was gone, I had to remind myself to breathe. Was Eli flirting with me? It seemed as if he was, but I could've been reading too much into it. There was no way to be sure. As I walked to my locker, I decided that whether he was or not, I had to make sure Billy didn't find out about it because I was *not* having a repeat of the Tyler Ferguson incident. Shuddering at the memory, I went to cross-country practice.

When practice was over, I met Billy behind the gym. I was sweaty and tired but still happy. There was something satisfying about staying in shape.

Billy cast a sideways glance at me as we walked to the car. "You're in an awfully good mood for it to be progress report day."

I shrugged. "I've had a good day. And that includes my progress report. How's yours?"

"Decent," he said. "I've got a D in Physics, but everything else is OK."

I patted his arm. "Grandpa knows you've been working hard. I doubt he'll be mad."

"That's true," he said, "but you never can tell how he'll—"

He stopped abruptly, so I looked at him to see what was wrong.

Billy was staring toward the car, scowling.

When I followed his gaze, I understood.

James was leaning against the car, which in itself wasn't unusual. Since he still refused to ride the bus, James waited by the car for us every day. But today, something wasn't right. His shoulders were hunched over, and he looked angrier than I'd seen him in a long time.

"Hey," James said when we walked up. Without looking at either of us, he tried to get in the car, which was still locked. With an aggravated sigh, he looked at us. "What?" he asked in a tone of barely forced calm.

"You tell us," Billy said.

James shook his head.

"What's wrong, James?" I asked.

When he didn't respond, I reached in my backpack for a notebook and pen.

"Can we please not do this right now?" he practically yelled.

I took my hand out of my bag, confused. The last couple weeks, he'd liked it when we made sure he understood us.

"Was it Austin?" Billy demanded. "Or someone else? Tell me who it was, and I'll—"

"Just drop it, OK?" James clenched his fists. "It's not something you can handle for me."

Billy didn't look convinced, but he unlocked the car. They both got in, and despite feeling that it might be safer to walk, I forced myself to do the same. As Billy cranked the car and drove out of the parking lot, I cast several furtive glances toward the backseat. I was stunned by James's anger. Grandpa had warned us that the phases of grief overlapped, but he'd seemed so much calmer lately. Maybe—

"I'm failing math," James said, cutting off my thoughts.

"What?" Billy and I said in unison. We both turned around to stare at him in shock.

"Watch the road, Billy," I ordered, pushing his head so it faced the front. "What do you mean you're failing math?" I asked James.

He continued as though I hadn't spoken. "And Mr. Vargas wrote Grandpa a note saying that I'm not paying attention and need to try harder. As if I'm not." He stopped abruptly and shook his head. He looked as though he wanted to hit something, and I couldn't blame him. In all the years we'd been in school, Grandpa had never received a note like that about any of us. There had been quite a few notes about Billy's conduct and maybe one or two about mine when I was in classes with Jenny. But never anything like this.

"It'll be OK, James," I said, unsure what else to tell him. "Grandpa will—"

"Save it, Ally," he snapped.

I froze, tears springing to my eyes.

James took a couple of deep breaths. "I'm sorry," he said in a softer tone. "I didn't mean...I'm just too upset to try to figure out what you're saying, OK?"

I nodded and turned back to face the front.

No one spoke until we got home.

We all entered the house grimly.

Grandpa was cooking supper when we came in, but after one look at our faces, he took the pot from the burner and pointed toward the living room. We went in and sat down.

"What's wrong?" Grandpa asked as soon as we were seated. He reached for the white board we now kept on the coffee table to write down the question.

"I understood you," James said before he even touched it.

Grandpa nodded and waited for one of us to speak. After a few tense seconds, James took a ball of crumpled paper out of his pocket and handed it to Grandpa, who straightened it out and read it. When he finished, he sighed and reached for the white board.

"Mr. Vargas says you're not paying attention and need to try harder," he wrote.

"I know," James said. "I read it."

Grandpa frowned at his belligerence but didn't comment on it. Instead, he wrote on the white board and turned it to face James as he read what he'd written aloud. "You've been through a lot," Grandpa said. "It's understandable that you're having trouble paying attention and trying hard."

"Having trouble," James repeated slowly, "trying hard." Suddenly, he stood up, snatched the note, crumpled it up again, and threw it across the room. "I am trying hard!" he roared in a tone I had never heard from him before. "I'm trying harder than I have ever tried in my life! I have no idea what's going on in any of my classes! I sit at the front, try to follow what the teacher's saying, and then piece together what I need to know using someone else's notes and the textbook. You want to know why I'm failing math? Because the stupid man doesn't *use* a textbook! He makes up his own stupid problems and turns his back to the class as he works them on the board! And then my stupid note-taker just copies down the problems with a few stupid arrows that are supposed to help me understand what to do. No one could learn like that! No one!"

We all stared at him with absolutely no clue how to respond, but James wasn't finished. He grabbed the remote and turned on the TV. Then he removed the captions we perpetually had on and pressed the mute button.

"What are they saying?" he demanded.

We all stared at the TV where a mom in a log cabin seemed to be giving her daughter a lecture. Or maybe she was teaching her how to do something or discussing the weather. It was impossible to know.

"Go on. Tell me. What are they saying?" James said. "Surely one of you can read their lips." He waved his hand at the screen. "Oh, look, she turned her back to the camera. What's she saying now?"

None of us answered. We just stared at him, completely dumbfounded.

"You don't know, do you?" he asked, his voice breaking. "Well then maybe you should pay attention and try harder. That'll fix the problem, don't you think?" He took a shuddering breath.

"It doesn't fix the problem, does it?" he asked quietly. "You know what does?" He pressed the mute button again and sound came pouring out of the TV. "What are they saying now?" he asked. "Do you understand them now?" He shook his head. "Because I don't. I have no idea what they're saying." He turned off the TV and stared at us.

"So, what am I supposed to do?" he asked. "There's no magic button to fix my problem, so how am I supposed to understand?" He sat on the couch and looked beseechingly at Grandpa. "What am I supposed to do?"

"I'm sorry, James," Grandpa said. "I didn't mean to—"

"I don't want you to be sorry," James said, his voice strangely calm now that his tirade was over. "I want you to answer my question. What am I supposed to do?"

Grandpa heaved a sigh. "I don't know."

"Neither do I," James said, "but paying attention and trying harder isn't it." Without even glancing at us, he got up and walked to his room.

Billy looked at Grandpa. "He's right about Mr. Vargas. He teaches by working problems on the board and explaining them as he goes. The class just follows along with him."

Grandpa nodded. "I'll set up a conference with him. I'll explain the problem and see if there's any way he could work with James individually. If not, I could try to find him a tutor. I don't know what else I can do." Looking distressed, he got up and walked to the kitchen to continue cooking supper.

"I've got a lot of homework." Billy grabbed his backpack. He took a couple steps toward his and James's room before rethinking his decision. "I think it's a lovely day to do homework on the porch."

We both smiled at his pitiful excuse, knowing full well he was just giving James some space, and then he left.

I sat on the couch trying to process everything James had said. *What are they saying? Surely, one of you can read their lips...*

I grabbed the remote, turned the TV back on, and muted it. For the next half hour, I watched the show and did my best to understand what was going on. By the end, I was ready to throw something at the TV. I was able to follow the general plot of the episode by watching the action, but I had no idea what was being said. Once in a while, I caught a word or two on someone's lips or filled in what I thought someone had said based on context, but I was never positive I'd gotten it right. It was galling.

As the credits rolled across the screen, I tried to imagine what it would be like to sit through all of my classes and have it feel like that. To understand only a few words the teacher said and have to fill in the gaps myself. My conscience forced me to admit I probably wouldn't last a day doing that. I already found most of my classes boring, but taking away the sound would make them unbearable. Yet, somehow, James had done it for four and a half weeks without complaining until today when Mr. Vargas's note had sent him over the edge. Now that I thought about it, James's tirade seemed not only justified, but downright reasonable. His final question haunted me though. What was he supposed to do?

I thought about it the whole evening and made no

progress. The next morning before school started, I told Missy all about what had happened. I was just expecting her to sympathize, but to my surprise, she did a lot more than that.

"It's not fair for James not to have the same opportunity to learn as everyone else," she said when I finished my tale. "There's bound to be something that can be done."

"Like what?" I asked with very little hope.

"I don't know," she said, "but something. If I've learned anything from my dyslexia, it's that if you want accommodations, you have to research, request, and sometimes demand them yourself."

"Accommodations?" I asked, completely at a loss.

She looked at me strangely. "Haven't you ever noticed that my tests are all on different color paper and that I go to a different room to take them?"

"Yeah," I said, still not sure where this was going.

"Well, those are some of my accommodations," she explained. "They're things that have to be done differently to help me learn."

After a moment, I nodded. That made sense. "What do you mean you had to demand them?" I asked. "Shouldn't teachers want to do whatever they can to help you?"

"Most teachers mean well." Missy shrugged. "But they don't always know what's best. After I was diagnosed with dyslexia, the special ed teacher said I needed to have all my tests read aloud to me, but my mom wanted me to be able to read on my own. She did research and had me try a lot of things at home to figure out what worked best for me. When she told the school what accommodations I needed, she had to fight to get them to agree."

"Really?" I asked. "You never said anything."

She shrugged. "It's not something I like to talk about, and I've never had a reason to bring it up until now." The bell rang, and she stood up, her expression determined. "I'll do some research about James's situation tonight and let you know what I find."

"OK," I told her, although I had serious doubts that she would find anything. Surely, if there were accommodations that could help James, the school would have already made them. Right?

Wrong. Missy showed up the next morning with a stack of papers she'd printed from several different websites. They described a wide array of accommodations James might qualify for. I sorted through the pile, feeling overwhelmed.

"I printed everything I thought could be even slightly useful," Missy said. "I thought maybe James could look through them at lunch today and see what he thinks."

I nodded, still a bit shocked at the sheer volume of information she'd brought. How could she have possibly found all of this so quickly? I considered asking her, but the bell rang before I had the chance.

I was distracted throughout the morning. Showing James Missy's research meant admitting that I'd told her about his F in math, the note from Mr. Vargas, the eruption—I mean, *expression*—of his feelings. I wasn't sure how he'd react.

Missy looked excited when we met for lunch. I felt queasy. By that time, I'd convinced myself that James would be furious with me and that he might even blow up again, or worse, be really hurt. I didn't eat a single bite of my lunch while we waited to see if James would join us. He did.

As soon as he sat down, Missy pulled out a notebook and pen. As James and Missy exchanged greetings, I gathered my courage.

"Ally, are you OK?" James asked, eyeing me with concern. "You have your 'I want to tell you something, but I don't know how you'll react' look on your face."

If I hadn't been dreading our conversation so much, I would have smiled. At least some things never changed.

"Don't be mad at me," I said, trying not to plead.

Missy quickly jotted that down in her notebook and held it up.

"Why would I be mad at you?" James asked.

When I didn't respond right away, he glanced at Missy, who looked as confused as he did. When she looked at me questioningly, I held out my hand in a silent request for the notebook and pen. She handed both of them to me, and I wrote the following message:

"I told Missy about your problems in math class." I held it up for James to see and braced myself.

He read it and then looked at me. Other than his cheeks turning slightly pink, he didn't seem upset. "She's your best friend, Ally. I'm not surprised you told her. But why are you telling me this right now?"

"Because I have some suggestions that might

help," Missy said, pulling the stack of papers out of her backpack. She handed them to James, who flipped through them curiously while I did my best to read them upside down. Professional note-takers, oral interpreters, sign language interpreters. I glanced at Missy.

"He doesn't know sign language," I told her.

She shrugged. "I told you I printed everything that he might find useful," she said, turning back toward James. I did the same and noticed he was reading one paper intently.

"Captionist," I read and looked at Missy. "What's that?"

"It's a person who types everything that's being said," she said, a satisfied smile on her face. "I thought he might like that one."

James reached the bottom of the paper and looked at her. "They have people who do this? They could actually caption my classes?"

"According to the website," Missy said with a nod.

"That would be awesome," James said, "but I doubt we have anyone who could do that around here."

Missy considered that. "Probably not, but maybe in Monroe." She wrote the word *Monroe* in the notebook. James seemed to contemplate that for a second.

"Do you really think I could get something like this?" he asked. The combination of hope and desperation in his voice broke my heart.

Grabbing the notebook from Missy, I wrote and

said with determination, "Only one way to find out."

After supper that night, James asked to speak to Grandpa alone. As the two of them walked to the porch, I gave James a thumbs-up and mouthed good luck.

Billy watched us, puzzled. "What's going on?" he asked me as soon as the door shut.

I summarized our lunch conversation for him. His face grew angrier and angrier the longer I spoke.

"They have stuff like that?" he demanded when I finished. "Why hasn't the school gotten it for him before now?"

"Maybe they didn't know," I said, trying valiantly to give them the benefit of the doubt. "Missy said the teachers here didn't know how to handle her dyslexia. Maybe they don't know how to handle deafness either."

"It can't be that hard to find out," Billy argued. "Missy found tons of information in one night. I bet none of his teachers even looked."

"Neither did we," I pointed out.

He frowned and seemed to deflate a little. "You're right. I'm glad Missy had the sense to look."

"Me, too," I said and walked over to the sink to start washing dishes.

The window over the sink looked out over the porch, not that that had anything to do with my desire to do the dishes right away. Everyone knows it's better to wash dishes quickly to prevent the food from sticking.

Billy came over to help me dry. "Can you tell how

it's going?"

"No," I said in disgust. "I can't tell at all."

James came back in just as we put away the last plate.

"Well?" I asked.

He smiled halfheartedly. "Grandpa says he'll call the school tomorrow and ask about getting a captionist for me. I'm trying not to get my hopes up too high, though. They could say no."

I nodded but let my hopes soar. I was sure the school would say yes. If it would help a student succeed, they had to. Right?

Wrong. When we came home from school the next day, Grandpa told James via dry erase board that the special ed teacher said that the school couldn't provide a captionist for him but that he was welcome to stay for tutoring after school if he needed extra help.

James tried to hide his disappointment, but it didn't really work. He went for a walk a few minutes after their discussion.

Grandpa watched him go. He looked older than I had ever seen him.

I wanted to cry but decided it would be a waste of saltwater. Instead, I called Missy.

"They said what?" Missy yelled when I told her.

I jumped and held the phone away from my ear.

"That's absurd! What are you going to do?"

"I guess James will stay after school for tutoring," I said, not seeing any other option.

"Ally, that's ridiculous," she said. "He doesn't need a tutor. He needs to know what his teachers are saying during class."

"I know that. But what are we supposed to do? Grandpa talked to the special ed teacher, and she said the school can't provide a captionist for him."

"Well, she's wrong," Missy interrupted. "Legally, the school has to provide reasonable accommodations. And for a deaf student, that has to include a way to know what's being said in class. Did he show her the information that I gave you?"

"I don't think so. He talked to her over the phone."

She was quiet for a few seconds, and I could practically hear the wheels spinning in her brain. At last, she said, "I think he should try talking to the school again, in person this time."

"What good will that do?"

"I doubt anyone in this school district has ever had a captionist before, so maybe the special ed teacher he talked to just hasn't heard of it. So, if he can show her or someone else at school the information, maybe they'll change their mind."

"I don't know. If they already said no…"

"The school said no when my mom first told them what accommodations she wanted me to have. My mom had to request an IEP meeting, and—" She stopped abruptly. "Actually, can you hold on just a minute?"

"OK," I said, unsure what was going on. I heard Missy and her mom talking but couldn't make out what they were saying. Then, Missy came back over the line. "Could my mom and I come over tonight?"

I gave the phone the puzzled look I wanted to give

her, hoping maybe she could sense my confusion. "I don't know. It's a school night, and we haven't really had people over since—"

"Please, Ally. I think it would really help if my mom could talk to your grandpa in person."

That was the second time she'd interrupted me in one conversation, which meant she believed this was extremely important.

"I'll ask Grandpa. Give me a minute." Setting the phone down, I went in search of him.

Grandpa was reluctant to let Missy and her mom come at first, but when I told him it was about James, he acquiesced.

"He says you can come after supper," I told Missy. "Would seven o'clock be OK?"

"Seven's fine. See you then."

I hung up still feeling bewildered.

Supper that night was a somber affair. James had been quiet during meals for months. Trying to eat and follow conversation at the same time was challenging for him, but he'd told us he didn't mind if we talked. Normally, the rest of us chatted to our hearts' content. But not that night. Grandpa sat with his shoulders hunched and his eyes downcast the entire meal. I was preoccupied, wondering what Missy or her mom could say that would help the situation, which left Billy no one to talk to even if he wanted to. It was more than a little pathetic.

Missy and her mom showed up right at seven. I opened the door before they had a chance to knock.

"Hi, Ally," Ms. Cathy said. "I haven't seen you in

a while."

"Hi, Ms. Cathy," I said. "Yeah, things have been pretty busy around here." I glanced at Missy, unsure what else to say.

Thankfully, Grandpa chose that moment to walk up behind me. "Hi, Cathy. Come on in."

"Actually, I was wondering if you might join me on the porch," Ms. Cathy said. "That way we can talk without any interruptions."

"Sounds good."

Ms. Cathy smiled and walked over to sit in one of our rocking chairs with Grandpa on her heels.

Missy came inside and shut the door.

"What does she need to tell him that's such a secret?" I asked, doing my best not to scowl.

Missy rolled her eyes. "It's not a secret. It's just a bit technical. I'll give you the simple version while they talk."

"All right." I led her into the living room. When we were both seated on the couch, I raised my eyebrows. "Well?"

"Basically, there's a law that says the school has to provide appropriate accommodations for students with disabilities. Mom's telling your grandpa how she convinced the school to give me what I needed, even after they refused at first."

I tilted my head. "How did she convince them?"

"I don't know." Missy shrugged. "When I asked, she told me not to worry about it."

"Gotcha." It sounded like something Grandpa would say, too.

We sat in comfortable silence for a few minutes until Missy broke it. "What's this?" she asked, picking up a book from the shelf under the coffee table. "I thought you said James doesn't know sign language."

I looked at the book in question. It was a book James's therapist had given him over the summer titled *American Sign Language: An Introduction*. She'd given him several books about the ways that people with hearing loss communicate.

"He doesn't," I said. "I mean he might've learned a little bit from that book but not enough to understand an interpreter."

"I know that," Missy said, "but—"

"Missy!" her mom yelled from the porch. "Time to go!"

Missy set the book back where she'd found it. "See you tomorrow, Ally." She headed for the door.

"See you. And thanks for asking your mom to help. I'm sure Grandpa will be able to convince the school to give James a captionist now."

"I hope so. The school system might still put up a fight, but at least he'll have something to fight back with." On that encouraging note, she left.

I wasn't worried, though. Surely, the school would be reasonable when presented with a law. Right?

Wrong. At that point, I officially stopped giving the school system the benefit of the doubt. Grandpa had to fight hard to get a captionist for James. He didn't share the details, but it took a lot of meetings with several different people before the school finally gave in. Finally, when the first nine weeks was almost over, a woman from Monroe came to our school and captioned James's classes every day. My middle cousin's relief was palpable, and his grades and attitude improved dramatically during the second nine weeks. Apparently, knowing what his teachers said actually helped him learn. What a radical concept. Cough cough...Mr. Vargas...cough cough!

All of that was settled just in time for us to get caught up in the homecoming buzz that swept through the school in mid-October. Clubs and sports teams started decorating their floats about two weeks before the homecoming festivities. As a member of the cross-country team, I spent hours painting, taping, and cutting, trying to make our float the very best.

During school hours, all anyone could talk about was who would go to the dance with whom. For the seventy billionth time, I wished Billy wasn't so overprotective. I would have loved to go to the dance with a certain guy from my homeroom, but I knew better than to hope for it. As far as I knew, Billy's feelings about my dating hadn't changed, and I liked Eli too much to risk getting him beaten to a pulp by asking him myself. I considered going to the dance alone but decided against it. Most of my friends from cross country had dates, and Missy hadn't shown any interest in going. Being the only person flying solo would be even lonelier than staying home with James and Grandpa, and Jenny would never let me hear the end of it.

On Monday, a week before homecoming, I met Missy for lunch as usual.

"I want to talk to you about something," she said as we got in line.

"OK. What's up?"

"I've been thinking about going to the homecoming dance."

I felt my eyes widen in surprise. Freshman year, she'd refused to even consider going.

"Really?" I asked, trying to keep any trace of incredulity out of my voice.

"Yeah. See, there's a guy I want to go with, but I don't think he'll ask me...so I think I might ask him."

I stared at her, stunned. She could have told me that she'd decided to move to Antarctica to study penguins, and I would have found it more likely than what she'd just said. Missy was one of the shyest people I'd ever met. I wasn't sure I'd ever seen her so much as make eye contact with a guy. Well, she talked to James at lunch, but that didn't count. How did she possibly think she would work up the nerve to ask a guy to the homecoming dance?

"Wow." I knew she could hear my disbelief. "That's…" Misguided? Insane?

"I know it's a little out of character. But I've liked this guy for a really long time, and I think he might like me, too. But I doubt he'd even think about asking me to the dance."

I frowned. It sounded as though she'd talked to this guy before. Had she gotten to know him in one of her classes this year and not mentioned it?

"So, who is this guy?" Curiosity got the better of me.

Missy gnawed her lower lip nervously. "That's kind of what I wanted to talk to you about."

I got a sick feeling in the pit of my stomach.

"It's Eli, isn't it?" I tried not to sound too hurt. Missy knew how much I liked him. How could she—?

"What? No, of course not. I would never do that to you."

I sighed in relief. "Then who?"

She took a deep breath. "James." She didn't meet my eyes.

Surprise coursed through me, followed by amusement. Apparently, James did count.

"Well, if you like James, you should ask him," I told her firmly. "And you're right. I doubt he's thinking about going to the dance at all, much less asking someone."

She studied me. "You're not mad?"

"Of course not. Why would I be?"

"I don't know. I've always thought you might—"

"Always?" I interrupted. "How long have you liked him?"

She pondered that for a second. "Probably since the first time I came to stay at your house."

I gaped at her. "Missy, that was in third grade. You've liked him all this time and never said anything?"

She nodded and turned bright pink.

"Well, you should have told me," I informed her, "because I could've helped get the two of you together."

She smiled but still looked unsure. "You're really

not mad?"

"Nope. Not even a little bit." By this time, we'd reached the kitchen where we got our food.

"Good." She grabbed a tray with something that might have been red beans and rice on it. "Then I'll ask him today if he sits with us."

I felt the corners of my mouth turn up as I got my own tray. How could Missy have kept her crush a secret for so long? And how could I have not noticed? Deciding that I needed to be more observant, I followed Missy to our table.

James still sat with Missy and me fairly often at lunch, and today, once he got his food, he headed our way. Missy looked terrified as he walked toward us, and I was afraid she'd lose her nerve if she had too long to think about it. As soon as James sat down, I got his attention.

"Missy has a question for you," I told him, writing it in the notebook as well.

When James looked at her quizzically, Missy darted her gaze to me, her expression panicked. I gave her a go-for-it nod, and she took a deep breath.

I expected her to reach for the notebook, but she didn't. Instead, she lifted her hands and did what I could only assume was sign language as she said, "Do you…want to go…to the dance…with me?"

James stared at her for a second, and then he smiled. Not a half-smile or a smile to hide pain, but a real smile. The first one I'd seen on his face since last May. Then, he simultaneously said and signed, "Yes."

11

—GOOD SIGNS

I'm not entirely sure how I made it through my classes the rest of the day. My thoughts just kept bouncing back and forth between the fact that Missy was James's date to the homecoming dance—which blew my mind—and the way she'd asked him. I wasn't an idiot. James had been glad that she'd asked him, but part of his happiness had come from *how* she'd asked him. Missy had used sign language, and James had understood her easily. That meant he knew at least some signs.

My thoughts went back to the book Missy had found under the coffee table. James must have been learning to sign for quite a while without mentioning it to us. The more I thought about it, I decided he must have gone out of his way to hide it. That was the only way none of us would have noticed him practicing. But why?

When I met Billy outside the gym after practice, I decided to give him the most monumental news first. "Guess what?"

"Your science teacher was abducted by aliens and replaced with a clone?" When I glared at him, he shrugged. "You told me to guess."

I rolled my eyes. "James and Missy are going to the homecoming dance together."

"Seriously?"

"Of course, seriously," I snapped. "Why would I joke about something like that?" Honestly, he made no sense sometimes.

"That's great. I wonder why James didn't tell me he planned to ask her. I didn't think he'd even want to go to the dance this year."

"He didn't ask her. She asked him."

Billy stared at me incredulously. "Missy Carver. Your best friend, one of the shyest people to ever walk the earth, asked James to the dance?" When I nodded, he whistled. "And you thought my alien theory was far-fetched. I mean, I knew she liked him, but—"

"You knew?" I interrupted, outraged. "How did you know she liked him? I didn't even know!"

He shrugged as if it wasn't important. "She looked at him different than she looked at me."

I glared at him. He wasn't supposed to know things about my best friend that I didn't. "How long have you known?" If he said "since third grade", I would punch him in the face.

"Since you were in middle school," he said.

I scowled but didn't hit him. "Why didn't you tell me?"

He gave me a strange look. "I would think that would be obvious." When I continued to glare at him, he rolled his eyes. "She's your best friend, Ally. I assumed you knew." With that, he strolled toward the car.

I was so aggravated that it drove everything else from my mind as I followed him. It wasn't until the ride home, as Billy tried and failed to have a conversation with James while driving, that I remembered Missy signing to him. When Billy gave up on talking to James, I turned around and looked at him.

"What's up with the sign language?" I asked him.

Both of my cousins gave me a puzzled look, so I pulled out my notebook.

"What are you talking about?" Billy asked.

"Missy asked him to the dance using sign language," I explained while writing my original question in the notebook. When I finished, I showed it to James.

"The therapist gave me a sign language book," he said, as if that explained everything.

"And?" I asked.

"She recommended that I learn some signs. She thinks it's the most accessible communication method for the profoundly deaf." He said the last part as if he were quoting directly from a textbook.

"So, why haven't we seen you practicing?" I asked and wrote. He read it and then looked out the window in a way that would have seemed casual if I didn't know him so well.

"I don't know. I guess I practice when I'm by myself."

"Why?"

He shrugged one shoulder.

"Why?" I repeated.

He looked out the window again. "I didn't want you to think you needed to learn it or that I'm different or anything." He looked uncomfortable.

I decided to let the subject drop for the moment. "I see." I turned back to face the front.

Billy shot me a questioning look from the driver's seat.

I shook my head and mouthed "later."

Billy suppressed a laugh, his eyes dancing with amusement. It took me a second to figure out why. I'd mouthed the word rather than saying it aloud because I didn't want James to *hear* me...I shook my head and wondered how long it would be before I stopped doing these types of things.

When we got home, Grandpa was in the kitchen cooking supper. Bless his heart. With three teenagers to feed, two of them boys, the man seemed to always be cooking something.

"How was school?"

"Good," James said.

Grandpa dropped the spoon he was holding in surprise. Even since getting a captionist, James hadn't described a single day positively this year.

"Missy asked me to go to the homecoming dance with her," James said and headed for his room.

Grandpa watched him go. "You know, I've never thought about it, but I could see James and Missy being good for each other. I'm glad she asked him. He never would've asked her or anyone else now that he's deaf."

"She asked him using sign language," I told Grandpa.

"So, what's the deal with the sign language, Ally?" Billy cut in. "You gave James the third degree about it on the way home."

"I don't know exactly. But when Missy asked James to go to the dance, he smiled. A real smile. The kind he used to get when he played the guitar. I know he was excited she asked him, but I think he also liked the way she asked him."

Grandpa looked thoughtful.

I could tell what I'd said about James smiling had hit home.

"The therapist mentioned that she'd given him a sign language book," Grandpa said. "And she suggested that we might want to study it with him, but when I asked James about it, he said he wasn't interested."

"In the car, he said he'd been practicing on his own," Billy said. "That he didn't want us to look at him differently…"

"Or think we have to learn it," I completed for him.

"But that doesn't make any sense," Billy said. "If signing makes it easier for James to communicate, we'd all *want* to learn it. Doesn't he know that?"

Grandpa sighed. "James has always done everything in his power to not be a burden on any of us. It's been one of his biggest obstacles since losing his hearing."

"That's true," I said. "It's taken him months to be OK with not understanding what we say, and even now, he still apologizes occasionally, like it's a huge inconvenience for us to repeat it or write it down."

"We should talk to him about sign language and see what he says," Billy suggested in his take-charge tone. "How about tonight after supper?"

Grandpa nodded his agreement.

"Plan made," I said with finality and went to my room to start my homework.

As we ate supper that night, I wondered how best to get James into the living room once we finished eating. If we could get him there, it would be pretty easy to bring up Missy signing to him, which would naturally lead into the conversation we wanted to have. James would never suspect we'd planned it beforehand. Getting him there was the tricky part. James almost always went to his room, or occasionally to the porch, to work on homework after supper. I considered asking him to help me with my homework, but since I didn't actually need help, that would make him suspicious. Try as I might, I couldn't come up with any other ideas. By the time we started putting away our dishes, I was getting desperate. Maybe I could—

"James," Billy said, patting him on the arm, "go to the living room. We want to talk to you." He pointed in the direction of the living room to get his point across.

Raising his eyebrows, James did as he asked. I rolled my eyes. When all else failed, you could always count on Billy to use the direct approach.

"What?" Billy demanded, seeing my expression.

"You don't win any points for subtlety," I informed him.

Now it was his turn to roll his eyes. "Do I win points for getting him into the living room to talk with us?" he asked. "Because your *subtlety* certainly wouldn't have."

I glowered at him but said nothing. He had a point after all.

Without another word, we walked into the living room.

Grandpa put down the cloth he was using to wipe the table and followed us.

James was sitting on the couch, his expression carefully blank. I got the feeling he knew, or at least suspected, what we wanted to talk to him about and wasn't particularly excited about it. The other three of us sat down, and Grandpa grabbed the dry erase board.

"Missy asked you to the dance using sign language." He wrote and held it up.

James nodded but said nothing.

Grandpa erased the board and continued. "Ally says you understood her and seemed to like it."

James read it and nodded, his lips still clamped shut. He was not making this easy.

"Do you like signing?" Grandpa asked using the board.

James read it but didn't respond right away. He glanced at each of us and then looked down at his lap. "I guess," he said finally.

Billy waved to get him to look up. "What does that mean?" He reached for the board.

"The therapist recommended I learn to sign,"

James said before Billy could uncap the marker. "So I've been studying it some."

"When?" I asked. "I've seen the book, but I've never once seen you look at it."

"What?" James asked.

"When?" I repeated slowly.

He shrugged. "Now and then."

"When you're by yourself," Billy corrected.

James wasn't looking at him, so he never knew Billy spoke.

Grandpa wrote something and turned the board around.

"Why have you been hiding this from us?" he asked.

James frowned. "I wasn't hiding it exactly. I was just afraid if you saw me signing...you might think I wanted you to learn it too or...that I wouldn't understand you if you spoke to me."

I looked at the white board and back at him, confused. A lot of the time, he *didn't* understand us when we spoke to him.

"I know I don't always understand you," he said. "I just don't want that to stop you from talking to me. I was afraid if you saw me signing, you'd think that was the only way to communicate with me, and since you don't sign..." He wouldn't meet any of our eyes.

Despite his use of the past tense, I could tell that his fear was still very real. I stared at him, completely at a loss. How could he think there was anything that would keep us from talking to him?

Billy and I both reached for the dry erase board at

the same time, but Grandpa was ahead of us. He'd already started writing a response. When he finished, he spoke the words he'd written. "James." His voice was gentle but firm. "We love you, and we will do whatever it takes to communicate with you. If that means learning sign language, then we'll do it."

"You don't have to," James said. "I don't want—"

Billy held up a hand to stop him. "Have to?" he repeated in an aggravated tone. "Did it never occur to you that we might want to?"

"What?" James asked.

With a sigh, Billy grabbed the board from Grandpa and wrote down his question. After James read it, he looked genuinely confused. "Why would you want to?"

That was too much for me. I seized a throw pillow and threw it at his head. Caught off guard, it hit him squarely in the face.

Three pairs of eyes looked at me in shock.

"Because we love you and enjoy talking to you, you idiot!" I snapped.

"Ally," Grandpa began, but I wasn't finished.

"What if it was me?" I demanded. "What if I was deaf and you could hear? Wouldn't you want to do everything you could to communicate with me?"

James stared at me, confused. He obviously knew I was angry, but he had no idea what I'd said.

"I've got you covered, Ally," Billy said, holding up his left hand in a one-second gesture as he wrote rapidly on the dry erase board with his right. After a few seconds, he turned it for James to see. He'd written down everything I'd said, verbatim.

"How'd you do that?" I asked, impressed enough to get distracted from my outrage.

"I've got a good short-term memory," Billy said. "Once in a while, it comes in handy."

"Oh." I turned back to James with what I hoped was a piercing stare.

"Of course, I would," he said in response to my question. "I'd do anything to communicate with you…with any of you."

I sighed. "So, what makes you think we feel any different about you?" I asked.

Billy started to write it down, but James shook his head. "I got the gist," he said, "and I see your point. Although I think I could've seen it without being hit in the head with a pillow."

He tossed the throw pillow back at me, and I caught it, unrepentant.

Grandpa, meanwhile, had been writing on the dry erase board. "So, does sign language make it easier for you to communicate?" he asked, letting James read it.

"Yeah," James said. "At least I think so."

We all nodded.

Grandpa said, "Then, it's settled."

We spent the next half-hour learning the manual alphabet.

The next morning before school started, I told Missy all about our family conversation from the previous evening. She was excited that we all planned to learn sign language and suggested that the two of us practice together in our spare time. I was in a great mood until I got to my first class and saw Eli.

Now, don't get me wrong, I always enjoyed seeing Eli, but it also made me think about how much I wanted him to take me to the homecoming dance. And that reminded me that I was the only person I knew who wasn't going to the dance at all. I suppressed a sigh. Next Saturday, I would watch my cousins get ready and then sit at home with Grandpa, knowing they were out having a good time. It made me want to strangle someone, namely Billy.

I was so preoccupied with these thoughts that I jumped when Eli said my name. Trying to hide my embarrassment, I turned to look at him.

"I want to talk to you about something."

"OK," I replied. He could talk to me about anything he wanted, and I would at least pretend to find it interesting.

"I've heard your cousin is the guy who beat up Austin Peterson a few weeks ago."

I nodded. "Yep, that's Billy."

"I've also heard he's threatened to kill any guy who asks you out," he continued.

My heart fluttered wildly in my chest. I had the urge to pinch myself to see if this was really happening but resisted it. Instead, I nodded.

"Well, here's the thing. I want to take you to the homecoming dance, but I don't want to get beaten up. So, I was thinking I would talk to your cousin about it first. Before I do that, I want to know if you're interested in going with me. If you're not, there's no reason for me to risk getting turned into ground beef."

By this time, my heart was pounding so hard I was afraid he could see it through my shirt. Somehow, I managed to nod and say, "Yeah, I'm interested" in a very breathy voice. He grinned, and I smiled back at him, feeling giddy.

"Great," he said as Mr. Thompson started class.

My smile faded as I turned to face forward.

Please Lord, I prayed. *Please, don't let Billy kill him.*

I was a nervous wreck for the rest of the day. Missy and James could tell something was wrong at lunch, but I refused to tell them what it was. I just couldn't bear to talk about it, not until I knew the outcome.

During cross-country practice, I ran quite a bit faster than usual with the theory that I could outrun my anxiety. It didn't work. As I walked to meet Billy at the gym, I was dripping with sweat but still just as worried as before. Eli needed to talk to Billy soon, or he wouldn't have a homecoming date regardless of Billy's answer. The suspense would kill me.

Billy was waiting for me in the gym with a calculating look on his face. I knew instantly that Eli had talked to him but decided to wait for him to bring it up. If I seemed too eager, it might affect Billy's answer.

Fortunately, he didn't make me wait. "I had an interesting conversation with a boy named Eli today," he said as I walked up, his tone unreadable.

"Did you?" I asked, trying to look authentically surprised.

Billy nodded. "He asked for my permission to take

you to the homecoming dance." His lips quirked slightly at the end of this statement

My patience evaporated. "And what did you say?"

Billy paused for dramatic effect. "I told him he could take you to the dance..."

My heart soared.

"...if the two of you go out to eat with my date and me beforehand."

And then plummeted. What if Eli didn't want to double date with Billy? What if—?

"He said that would be fine."

I heaved a sigh of relief.

Billy looked at me reproachfully. "Eli said the two of you have been talking during homeroom since the beginning of the year. It would have been nice if I'd heard about him before now."

I narrowed my eyes. "Yeah? Well, it would have been nice if guys had been able to talk to me without being afraid of being beaten half to death for the last year. Sadly, that didn't happen either."

Billy's mouth twitched again. "That's fair," he said, walking toward the car.

Daydreaming about what my dress would look like, I followed him. I thought about the homecoming dance for the entire evening. And the more I thought about it, the more I was sure that going out to eat with just Billy and his date was a bad idea. I didn't think Billy would be *mean* to Eli, but he was bound to ask him awkward questions. That was unacceptable. Eli didn't deserve to be interrogated during dinner, which meant something had to be done to deter Billy. I wasn't sure who Billy was bringing as his date, so there was no guarantee of any help there. Since Eli would be the one on the spot, I would be the only one there to prevent disaster. Also unacceptable. I needed allies, and I knew exactly who they should be.

James and Missy would be the perfect people for the job. As my best friend, Missy would do everything she could to help me, and having James there would distract Billy just by giving him another guy to talk to. Even better than that, James could sit between Billy and Eli, thereby becoming a physical barrier between them as well.

As I lay in bed that night, I tried to decide how best to go about persuading them to join us. Should I talk to Missy first and try to convince her of how desperate my plight was? Should I talk to James and appeal to his protective instincts? Which way gave me the greatest chance of success? I had no idea. In the end, I decided to ask them together at lunch the next day, with the theory that it would be less nerve-racking for me to only explain the situation once.

When I finally fell asleep, I dreamed I was having a birthday party where Eli was the piñata, and Billy kept whacking him with a stick. When I tried to get Eli away from him, Billy pushed me away, claiming, "smart women didn't date until their thirties."

On Wednesday morning, I woke up more determined than ever to persuade Missy and James to go out to eat with us before the dance. When I arrived at school, I sat with Missy before the bell rang like I always did. I was dying to tell her about Eli asking me to the dance, but telling her would require explaining about him asking Billy, which would lead into Billy's stipulation. Overall, I knew it would be better if I kept the whole story to myself until lunch. I didn't know what else to talk about, though, so I didn't say anything. With me being...well, me...I knew that might be suspicious, but I just couldn't think of anything else worth mentioning.

"Ally, are you OK?" Missy asked after we'd stood without speaking for a while.

"I'm fine." I hoped she'd let the subject drop.

Of course, she didn't.

"You've been awfully quiet since Monday. Are you sure you're OK with James and me going to the dance together?" She looked extremely nervous, as if she wasn't sure what she would do if I said no.

"Positive."

"Well then, what's wrong?" she asked, looking legitimately concerned for my well-being.

I sighed. "Nothing," I told her. "I've just got something on my mind." As soon as I said it, I wished I could pull the words back into my mouth. I knew she'd never let me say that without asking...

"What?"

I considered making something up but decided against it. "Honestly, there's something I want to talk to you about, but I want to talk to you and James together."

She frowned, obviously thinking it was something serious.

"It's not anything bad," I assured her quickly.

"Just...I guess you'd call it a favor."

She cocked her head and studied me as if she could read my mind if she tried hard enough.

"OK," she said at last, and then thankfully, the bell rang.

Before our first period class began, Eli and I talked about the dance, and I told him about my plan to get James and Missy to go with us. He was fine with it but didn't seem too worried if it didn't work out. I shook my head. He clearly didn't know Billy very well.

Despite my attempts to focus only on my classes that morning, I was a nervous wreck by the time I went to lunch. Thankfully, Missy didn't ask me any questions while we waited in line, though I could tell she wanted to.

As it turned out, I was nervous for nothing. James and Missy were both glad that Eli had asked me to the dance and said they would be happy to join the four of us for dinner beforehand. From the looks on their faces, I got the impression that they'd been a little nervous about going out to dinner, just the two of them. Feeling proud, I congratulated myself on a very good idea.

Billy was pleased that James and Missy were joining us, too. He said it would be the last chance for all three of us to go to a dance together and that we should make the most of it. That was the first time I'd really thought about Billy graduating in May. It made me kind of sad, so I forced it to the back of my mind. This was a time for happiness.

On Saturday, Missy's mom took Missy and me to

the mall in Monroe to shop for dresses. Grandpa gave me money and wished me luck, obviously glad to be spared the ordeal of taking me shopping. After going to five different stores and trying on at least twenty dresses apiece, we both found ones we liked: knee-length and pink for me, floor length and navy blue for Missy, each with modest necklines. While we both believed in keeping ourselves covered, I also knew that all three of the males in my family would lock me in my bedroom before letting me leave the house in a dress that showed more than they felt was appropriate. And I was not taking any chances.

Homecoming week at our high school was a lot of fun. Each day had a theme, and we were allowed to wear clothes to match it. That year, we had pajama day, mismatch day, hero day, cowboy/cowgirl day, and school spirit day. I had outfits for all of them, but my favorite, by far, was my hero costume. It had a cape and everything.

On Friday night, Grandpa, James, and I went to the football game to support Billy. It was fun, except for half-time. Jenny was on the homecoming court, and I wanted to throw up as I watched her strut across the field on Tony's arm. Not because I was jealous, but because I held a firm belief that anything that gave Jenny bragging rights could never be a good thing. On the bright side, we won the football game, and Billy scored two touchdowns.

The homecoming parade was held on Saturday morning. Most of the parish showed up to watch, so we had a decent-sized crowd. I rode on the cross-country float and enjoyed pelting people with candy a little too much. Unfortunately, the parade barely lasted an hour.

Ms. Cathy had agreed to do my hair after lunch, but that left me with two hours to kill. I tried watching TV with Billy, but he kicked me off the couch after about ten minutes because I was bouncing my leg and glancing at the clock too much. Then I tried reading on the porch, but I just couldn't get into the plot of my book. Out of sheer desperation, I attempted to work on my algebra homework, which was a complete and utter disaster, given my lack of concentration.

At long last, it was time for lunch. I practically inhaled my sandwich and then tapped my fingers on the table impatiently as Grandpa methodically chewed and swallowed. I'd seen cows eat faster than that, which is sad considering that they have to chew their food twice before it can be digested.

When Grandpa finished his two never-ending sandwiches, he drove me over to Missy's. It took Ms. Cathy about two hours to curl and pin our hair, but somehow it was easier to wait knowing that the process of getting ready had officially begun. It also helped that Missy was equally, if not more, excited than I was.

Ms. Cathy brought me home that afternoon, promising to come back and pick up James around five. Since all of us wouldn't fit in Billy's car, she had generously offered to act as James and Missy's chauffeur for the evening. She would drop them off at the restaurant, drive them to the dance, and pick them up at the end. I would have liked to ride with them, but I didn't want to ask Ms. Cathy to pick up Eli, too. Therefore, with more than a little trepidation, I'd decided to ride with Billy. We planned to pick up Eli and Holly, Billy's date, and then meet James and Missy at the restaurant.

I put on my dress and did my makeup as soon as I got home. Then I put on my shoes, grabbed my bag, and looked at the clock. I almost banged my head on the wall in frustration. I might have actually done it if it wouldn't have jarred my hair loose of its pins. How could it possibly only be four o'clock?

Not wanting to be teased for being ready so early, I sat carefully on the edge of my bed and started reading one of my favorite fantasy novels, knowing that it wouldn't matter if I lost track of the plot since I'd read it several times already.

Thirty minutes later, I went and sat in the living room. It was my silent way of saying I was ready, and they should be, too.

James, who was almost ready himself, heard me loud and clear. Billy, however, was completely deaf to it. The irony of that did not escape me, but I didn't find it the least bit funny.

Billy didn't even start getting ready until 4:45 PM. James, who was completely ready by that point, gave me a sympathetic, if slightly amused, smile. I stared at the clock and tried not to panic. Horrible scenes flashed through my mind of us being so late to pick up Eli that he'd decided we weren't coming or so late to the dance that they refused to let us in.

Ten minutes later, Billy came out of his room in his suit. He ran his fingers through his hair and then, with a wicked grin, asked if I was ready to go. The only thing that kept me from chunking a throw pillow at him was the fear that he might throw it back at me and somehow mess up my hair or makeup. I settled for shooting him a scathing look before practically running for the car.

We picked up Holly first, which meant I was displaced to the backseat. I didn't mind, though, because I knew I'd get to sit next to Eli as soon as we picked him up. When we reached Eli's house, his front door opened, and he came striding out toward the car. He wore a black suit with a pink tie to match my dress and looked way too good to be allowed. I got out of the car to greet him. When he saw me, he smiled warmly, and a shiver ran down my spine.

"You look beautiful, Ally," he said, holding out a plastic box containing a corsage. "May I?"

When I nodded shyly, he opened the box and slipped the corsage on my wrist. It was a pink rose with a silver ribbon and quite possibly, the prettiest thing I'd ever seen.

"Thank you," I told him, finding my voice. "You look very handsome. I—"

"Are you getting in the car any time soon?" Billy asked through the door I'd left ajar. "Or should I turn off the engine and let you chat?"

I blushed, but Eli laughed.

"You get in that side," he said. "I'll walk around."

The ride to the restaurant wasn't nearly as

awkward as I thought it would be. Holly, it transpired, was a good conversationalist. She kept Billy entertained, which meant he had no time to interrogate Eli. I would always be in her debt.

When we arrived at the restaurant, a small Italian place, we found James and Missy sitting on a bench outside. Together, we went inside, and the hostess led us to our seats. The boys all sat on one side of the table directly across from their dates. As I'd hoped, James was in the middle between Billy and Eli. James gave me a you're-welcome smile before disappearing behind his menu. Suppressing a grin, lest Billy catch on and try to change the seating arrangement, I followed suit.

Our waitress came up a few minutes later. She was a young, blonde woman with tired but kind eyes. "What can I get you to drink?" she asked, glancing around the table.

Missy looked at James and signed DRINKS.

James nodded to show his understanding.

Watching them, the waitress gasped. "I'll be right back," she said before jogging to the kitchen.

We all glanced at each other, puzzled.

The waitress came running back moments later and, with an ecstatic smile, handed James what seemed to be another menu. Looking at it more closely, I saw that it was written using Braille. With great difficulty, I managed not to do a face palm. Instead, I looked from the menu to the waitress and back to the menu, hoping she'd realize her mistake. She didn't.

Billy opened his mouth to speak but shut it

abruptly as the table trembled.

"Thank you," James told her without a trace of sarcasm in his voice.

I wasn't sure how he managed it.

"You're welcome," she shouted and then took our drink orders as if nothing had happened.

As soon as she walked away, we all burst out laughing.

"You were looking at Missy," Billy told James adding the sign LOOK. "You looked at the waitress. How could she possibly think you're blind? And she yelled, too." He shook his head in exasperation. "You should have let me say something."

James shook his head, although he still looked amused. "She was trying to help," he said with a doubtful look toward the kitchen where she'd disappeared.

"Mission not accomplished," Billy said, and we all went back to perusing our menus.

The rest of dinner passed without incident, except for the waitress shouting at James every time she spoke to him. Eli was pretty quiet throughout the meal, probably because he didn't know anyone at the table besides me. His silence didn't bother me. The less he talked, the less Billy would give him a hard time. Besides, we'd have plenty of time to talk at the dance.

When the waitress brought the checks, Eli insisted on paying for my meal. Not that I argued much. Billy and James were paying for their dates' meals, so I figured Eli would cover mine, though I had brought money just in case.

Missy called her mom when the waitress brought the checks, so she was waiting in the parking lot when we left the restaurant. Missy and James got in her car while the rest of us piled into Billy's. This time I was behind Billy, which was a mistake. Now, he could see Eli.

"So how many girlfriends have you had, Eli?" Billy asked abruptly as we left the parking lot.

My jaw dropped in shock.

"Three," Eli said in a resigned tone that said he'd been expecting this conversation.

"Three," Billy repeated with a nod. "That's a good number. Enough to be believable but not enough to make me think you're a player."

I closed my eyes in horror. This couldn't be happening.

"So, what exactly are your intentions toward my cousin?" Billy asked.

My neck and face got horribly warm. I opened my eyes and glared at the back of Billy's head.

Eli, however, remained calm. "I like her, and I plan to have a good time with her at the homecoming dance…while being a gentleman, of course."

"Of course," Billy said, somehow managing to make the words sound like a threat.

"I'd like to listen to some music," Holly interjected and without waiting for permission, she turned on the radio and cranked it loud enough that no one could converse easily. I had never been so happy to hear eighties rock music in my life. I glanced apologetically at Eli, who shrugged and gave me a half-smile.

I sighed, giddy with relief that he wasn't upset and then stared out the window, determined to make sure nothing like this happened for the rest of the night.

When we arrived at the school, I got out of the car quickly and stood as close as I could to Billy while the car separated us from our dates. "One more word, Billy," I whispered, "and I swear you will wake up with a snake in your bed one night very soon."

Billy eyed me shrewdly. I could tell he knew it was no idle threat. There were plenty of snakes in the woods behind our house, and he'd taught me not to be afraid of them years ago. Granted, he wasn't afraid of them either, but waking up with a snake in his bed still wouldn't be pleasant.

"Fine," he whispered back. He walked around the car to take Holly's arm as Eli came and took mine.

"What was that about?" Eli asked as we walked to the gym.

"Nothing important," I told him, unable to suppress a grin.

He laughed but didn't ask any more questions.

The homecoming dance was everything I hoped it would be. Eli and I danced to at least half the songs, and we sat and chatted with each other any time we needed a break.

Billy and Holly stayed on the dance floor almost the whole night, seemingly having a great time. Occasionally, I caught Billy keeping an eye on Eli, but he kept his distance. The threat of a reptile in someone's bed could be a very effective deterrent.

Missy and James had a good time, too, despite the

fact that they didn't dance for most of the night. Instead, they sat a table and talked, using a combination of sign language and written notes.

Eli and I had just finished dancing to an upbeat song when I spotted trouble.

Jenny was walking toward Missy and James, her intentions obviously sinister.

"Would you get me some punch?" I asked Eli. "I think I want to sit down for a while."

"Sure," he said.

As he headed for the punch bowl, I made a beeline for where Missy and James were sitting and got there just in time to hear the end of Jenny's comment.

"…so sweet of you to come with someone who's disabled, Missy, even if he was your only option."

Anger surged through my veins. I was about to give Jenny a piece of my mind when James turned and looked at Missy.

"Did she say something important?" he asked her aloud, his tone politely conversational. "I didn't hear a thing."

Missy looked at Jenny and then back into James's eyes. She shook her head. "No, nothing important."

James nodded and looked at the couples swaying to a slow song. "Would you like to dance?" he asked Missy.

She smiled sweetly and let him lead her onto the dance floor, neither of them giving Jenny so much as a glance.

I smiled, my anger replaced by satisfaction at the look on Jenny's face.

Then she turned to me and smirked cruelly. "Shame he can't hear the music," she taunted.

I surveyed James and Missy, who were gazing into each other's eyes as they rocked back and forth in the high school equivalent of slow dancing. "He seems to be doing fine to me," I told her smugly.

Anger kindled in her eyes for a moment, but she seemed to force it down.

"Where's your date?" she asked. "Did you scare him away?"

Eli chose that moment to come walking up, two cups of punch in his hands. "There was a line at the punch bowl." He handed me a cup. Then he noticed we weren't alone.

"Hi, I'm Eli," he said, "and you're...Jenny, right?"

Jenny stared at us for several seconds, unsuccessfully trying to hide her resentment, before stalking off without another word.

"Well, that was friendly," Eli said, frowning.

I smiled, feeling triumphant as I watched Jenny march to a table and sit down to sulk. Then, for the first time since the spider incident in second grade, I felt something other than loathing for Jenny. I felt sorry for her. Sorry that she needed to make Missy and me feel bad just to have a good time. Shaking my head to clear it of this new and confusing emotion, I turned to Eli. "I've changed my mind," I told him, setting down my punch. "I want to dance some more."

Ignoring his puzzled look, I took his punch, set it next to mine, and led him onto the dance floor. As we swayed gently back and forth, I felt truly content for the first time since James's accident, and I realized that even though I'd lost *my thing*, I still had everything that truly mattered.

12

—THE SONG REMAINS THE SAME

The rest of the year passed too quickly for my taste. Eli and I talked a lot, and he even came and ate supper at our house once. We never did officially date that year because of Billy, but that didn't bother me too much.

James and Missy, on the other hand, started dating in January. This time, James asked her.

As the end of the school year drew nearer, my anxiety started to grow. This was the last year Billy would be in high school with us, which meant everything would change. For a while, Billy refused to even consider going to college. He'd decided to become a firefighter, which didn't require a degree, and he said he'd had enough school to last a lifetime.

After several lengthy discussions with Grandpa, he changed his mind. Louisiana had a program that would pay for a student's education at an in-state public university if their grades were high enough. Billy qualified for it, and Grandpa convinced him that it would be silly to turn down a scholarship when he might need a degree at some point in his life.

Billy applied to several different schools. Personally, I hoped he would go to the one in Monroe so that he would be close by, but Billy had other plans. In March, he announced his intentions of attending a university in Baton Rouge, about three hours away from our house. Even though I knew it was a good school, I dreaded only seeing Billy once or twice a month. I wanted time to stop and let us stay young, happy, and together forever.

Of course, since I wanted time to slow down, it seemed to move even faster than usual. Before I knew it, it was almost time for final exams and Billy's graduation.

On the first Sunday in May, we went to church as usual. Lee came over to talk to me as I shook out my umbrella, just inside the church's door. April showers had brought May showers, instead of flowers.

"Hi, Lee," I said when he walked up.

"Hi, Ally. Could I talk to you for a minute?"

"Sure." I wondered why he looked nervous.

"Before I ask you this, Ally, I want your word that you won't give me your answer right away. I want you to pray about it and give me your answer next week."

"OK." I started to feel nervous myself. What could he possibly ask me?

"Senior Sunday is in two weeks."

I nodded. Our church always recognized the high school seniors the Sunday before graduation.

"All the seniors will be recognized during the church service and be given a small gift," he continued.

I nodded again, still at a loss as to why he was telling me things I already knew.

"I'd like you to sing the special music that

Sunday," he concluded.

I stared at him in disbelief. "Lee—"

"You said you wouldn't give me your answer until next week, remember?" I glared at him but forced my mouth shut. How could he ask me to do this?

"Hear me out, Ally." Lee put his hand on my shoulder.

It took a lot of effort for me not to jerk away from him.

"I think it would mean a lot to Billy if you sang for Senior Sunday, and the church would love to have a member of the youth group sing that day. It would make the whole service more special for everyone."

I stared at the floor, trying to deny the truth of his words. Billy would understand why I couldn't sing in front of the church. And surely, people wouldn't care if—

"Ally, I know what happened last time. And I have a pretty good idea why you don't want to sing, but please, pray about it this week, OK?"

"I will." Anything to get him to leave me alone. And just so I wasn't lying to a minister, I decided I would pray about it. I would tell God exactly why I wouldn't sing in church. He'd understand. He wouldn't want me to cause James any pain. With my resolve firmly intact, I took my seat for Sunday school. My resolve weakened substantially during lunch.

"I heard you're singing for Senior Sunday," Billy said as he served himself mashed potatoes.

"No, I'm not." I tried to remain calm. "Where did you hear that?"

"Ryan told me he heard Lee ask you this morning."

I grabbed a chicken leg and a biscuit.

"Well, yeah, he asked me, but I said no."

Billy knit his brow but had to swallow a mouthful of food before responding. "You said no? Why?"

I sighed deeply. Apparently, he didn't understand as well as I thought he would. "You saw what happened last time. You should know why."

Billy rolled his eyes. "That was one time. Are you saying you'll let one bad experience keep you from ever doing it again?"

"Maybe." I didn't meet his eyes as I scooped mashed potatoes onto my plate. I wasn't about to tell him about my decision never to sing again, not with James sitting at the table with us. Besides, Billy probably wouldn't understand anyway.

"Come on, Ally. It's my Senior Sunday."

I shook my head and reached for the green beans, hoping no one noticed that my hands were shaking. It was hard to say no to Billy, but I really didn't have a choice.

"Ally," Grandpa said, inclining his head toward me.

"Can we not talk about this anymore?" I asked, hating the understanding I saw in his eyes.

Grandpa nodded, and we fell silent. After a few seconds, I risked a glance at James, hoping he hadn't paid attention to our conversation.

Instead of being absorbed with his food, he was looking at me thoughtfully as he ate.

Not wanting to know how much he understood or guessed about what was going on, I only looked up when Grandpa asked me questions about Sunday school.

It was Billy's and my turn to do the dishes, so when we finished eating, everyone piled their plates in the sink and left us to it. Since I felt bad about refusing Billy's request, I volunteered to wash, so he could dry.

As I scrubbed mindlessly, I looked out the window at the rain that continued to fall in sheets and thought about what Billy had said at lunch. It bothered me that he'd tried to talk me into singing. Billy wasn't one for letting his emotions show, at least not those he considered unmanly. The fact that he'd tried to persuade me to sing meant that he would probably be disappointed if I didn't. I hated that, but I didn't see an alternative. I couldn't sing. I wanted to, but I just couldn't. And that was that.

When I finished washing the dishes, I walked out on the porch. James had gone there after lunch, and I was curious what he was doing outside in the nasty weather. I found him sitting in a rocking chair, gazing out at the garden. I waved my hand to get his attention. "What...are you...doing?" I asked slowly, signing each word, too.

He smiled slightly. "Listening to the rain."

I stared at him as if he'd lost his mind. We both knew he wasn't listening, and he would never listen to anything again.

"Come sit with me," he said, nodding his head toward the chair next to him.

Still giving him a bewildered look, I sat down. He didn't say anything for a minute. He looked out at the garden, and I followed his gaze. The rows he and Billy had worked so hard to weed were filled with water, and rain was pouring off the roof of the barn.

"I used to love to sit out here while it was raining," James said, his voice hushed. "I'd listen as the drops hit the roof, the barn, the ground, and imagine it was God playing a song for us...for me." He paused for a second, remembering.

Tears sprang to my eyes, but I blinked them away.

"A lot of people don't like the rain," he continued. "It makes the sky dark, and everything gets muddy and messy, but it's beautiful in its own way. And it's necessary. Without it, nothing would grow." He looked at me.

I knew he wasn't just talking about rain.

This time I couldn't hold back the tears. They trickled down my cheeks as he held my gaze. He reached over and squeezed my hand. "I couldn't see that at first, Ally. When I lost my hearing, all I could see was the bad: all the things I couldn't do and the things I would miss. I got so caught up in the darkness and the mud that I missed the song. I missed what God was trying to teach me because I was so confused...and angry." He shook his head.

"But you were there for me. You, Billy, Grandpa, Missy. You gave me space when I needed it. You were patient when I didn't understand and when I got angry. You're even learning to sign to communicate with me. You showed me that life keeps going and can still be good, even if it's different. And finally, I listened to God's song and let Him show me how He could use this for good."

I wiped my eyes but beamed at him. *This* was my cousin, the one I'd always depended on, the one I thought I'd never see again.

He ran his hand across his eyes. "The last time you sang at church. I was still confused and angry. You saw that when you were standing on stage, and you thought I was angry at you and that I didn't want you to do something I couldn't."

"James." I shook my head, but he cut me off.

"That isn't true. I wanted to be able to hear you, but I never wanted you not to sing. I never wanted to take your music—your voice—away from you." He looked me in the eye. "I'm sorry I made you think that."

I nodded, tears still cascading down my face.

He smiled. "I think you should sing for Senior Sunday. It would mean a lot to Billy, and—"

"I can't, James," I said, too upset to sign. "How can I sing when you can't hear me?"

I'm not sure how he understood me, but he did.

"Who do you sing for, Ally?"

"What?"

"Who do you sing for?" he repeated. "Do you sing for me? So that I can hear you? Or do you sing for God? To praise Him, to use the gift He gave you for His glory?"

I stared at him with absolutely no response to that. Who did I sing for?

"Think about it." James stood up and walked into the house.

I stayed where I was, contemplating his question. It wasn't until I was lying in bed that night that I was willing to admit the answer. For me. Every time I'd sung for an audience, I'd done it for me. So people could hear *my* voice and clap for *me*. I saw singing as *my* thing, but it wasn't. And it never should have been.

I'd had my priorities mixed up all along. Instead of begging God to help me find *my* thing, I should have been asking Him to reveal my part in *His* plan, to help me find the things *He* wanted me to do. Guiltily, I knelt beside my bed. *I'm sorry, Lord,* I prayed. *I'm sorry that I've used my talent for my own glory instead of Yours. I'm so sorry.*

Much to my surprise, I felt His forgiveness sweep through me. As sure as heaven, I knew my pride and selfishness were covered by the blood of Jesus. Then another thought occurred to me. Why was I surprised? I'd accepted Christ as my Savior when I was seven years old. I'd felt His conviction and forgiveness more times than I could count. Why was I surprised to feel Him now?

The answer came to my mind so swiftly that I knew God Himself showed me. Last May, I'd decided God wasn't listening. I'd asked Him to heal James, and He hadn't, at least not in the way I wanted. In a moment of clarity, I realized I hadn't *really* prayed much in the last year. I'd gone through the motions, both with people and by myself, but I'd stopped truly believing God was listening and would answer. *Lord, forgive me,* I prayed. *Forgive me for not trusting You.*

As soon as I prayed that, I felt a weight lift off my shoulders. I should've trusted God all along, regardless of the outcome. Wasn't there a verse somewhere in the Bible about God working all things for the good of those who love Him? Then I thought about Grandpa. He'd lost his wife, three sons, and all the other family members, but he still trusted God. And somehow, God had even worked that for good by bringing our family together.

Wiping my tears away, I heaved a deep sigh. *Now that we're talking again,* I told God, *would you like me to sing for Senior Sunday? I'd like to, but I'd hate for James to be completely left out. What do you think?*

I heard no answer, but that was OK. He would tell me eventually, and I could wait.

It was kind of hard to think about anything other than schoolwork during the next week. There were only two weeks left before final exams, and I stayed up late every night trying to finish all of the homework and projects that were due. Still, every night before I fell asleep, I asked God the same question: do You want me to sing for Senior Sunday?

By Saturday, I was sure of His answer, and on Sunday, I told Lee the good news. "Lee." I walked up to him after I wiped my shoes. "I've decided to sing on Senior Sunday."

"That's wonderful, Ally." He beamed at me. "I'm sorry if I pressured you, but I had a feeling you needed to do this."

"It's fine," I assured him. "Do you have a song in

mind for me to sing? I've tried to think of one that relates to graduation, but I haven't come up with anything."

"As a matter of fact, I do."

He pulled a CD out of his Bible and held it out to me.

"How did you know I'd say yes?" I asked, taking the CD.

"I didn't." He shrugged. "But sometimes, you just have to have faith."

I smiled as he walked away, but in the back of my mind, I felt as though I was forgetting something important.

While Missy and I stood in the lunch line the next day, I told her about me singing for Senior Sunday at church. When I finished explaining what it was, she looked contemplative.

"I'd like to come. I'd like to hear you sing and see Billy get recognized."

"And sit with James," I teased.

She giggled. "That, too."

"I'm sure we could swing by your house and…" I stopped abruptly as an idea struck me.

Missy looked at me in alarm. "Ally, what—"

"I just had an epiphany."

"A what?" she asked, looking utterly lost.

"An idea," I explained. "A brilliant idea."

"Ally, you're starting to scare me. What—"

"You should perform with me on Sunday." Excitement coursed through my veins. It was perfect. Why hadn't I thought of it before?

"What?" she almost yelled. "Are you insane? I can't sing, and I—"

"I don't want you to sing," I told her, unsure where she'd gotten that impression.

"But you just said—"

"I want you to sign."

She stared at me as if I'd grown a second head. "Are you crazy? I can't sign a whole song...especially not in front of a crowd of people."

"But if you sign. James will still be able to understand and enjoy the song. He won't feel left out."

Missy bit her lip. I could tell she was at least considering it.

"We could work on it together. I'll come over to your house to study, and we can take breaks and practice." The more I talked, the more I knew the plan was perfect.

"I don't know, Ally. I've never been good with crowds. I barely survived giving a speech to my English class."

I frowned. That was true enough. She'd barely eaten for days before her speech, and she'd somehow still managed to throw up afterward.

"This would be different," I argued. "You'd be signing. No one in the audience would know if you made a mistake."

She hesitated.

"Come on, Missy," I pleaded. "It would mean a lot to me, and I know it would mean a lot to James."

"Oh, all right."

I clapped my hands in anticipation and started

making plans.

"OK, I want to surprise James, so you can't tell him."

"What? Absolutely not!"

"Why not?" I demanded. It seemed like a good idea to me.

"James is my boyfriend. The first one I've ever had and the only one I think I'll ever want."

I raised my eyebrows.

"I won't lie to him!" she almost yelled.

"You won't have to lie. You won't have to tell him anything. I'll come to your house to study, and we'll take breaks and work on it."

"What about me coming to church with you?" she asked. "What am I going to tell him about that?"

"Tell him you want to come to hear me sing and see Billy honored. It's true. You said so yourself a few minutes ago."

"You have an answer for everything, don't you?" She sighed and threw up her hands. "Fine. I won't tell him, but I have a bad feeling about this plan."

"Oh, come on. You'll see. It will go off without a hitch."

And it did. On Monday night, I called Lee to let him know the change in plans. He thought it was an excellent idea—thank you, thank you, very much!

I went to Missy's house to study every night that week. Although I confided what we were doing to Grandpa, James never suspected a thing, not even when Missy told him she planned to go to church with us on Sunday.

By Saturday night, Missy and I had practiced the song so many times that my voice and her arms were tired. She said she wasn't sure the song was translated into proper American Sign Language, or ASL, but that it would get the point across. I assured her that James would love it.

On Sunday morning, Billy and I dressed up more than usual for church, and we both were ready fifteen minutes early. For once, Billy was as excited as I was.

"Thanks for singing today, Ally," Billy said while we waited.

I grinned. "Thanks for being such a great cousin. I don't know what we would've done without you all these years."

"You'd have been lost." He was falsely earnest. "Unsure what to do or—"

I hit him with a pillow, cutting him off.

He chuckled and then turned serious. "I'll come home to visit, Ally. Graduating doesn't mean I won't still be part of the family."

"I know," I told him, blinking rapidly. "Now, talk about something else before I smudge my mascara."

We picked up Missy on our way to church. She looked slightly pale but otherwise fine. If James noticed anything was amiss, he didn't let on. Somehow, we all managed to sit through Sunday school, although I doubt any of us knew what Lee said. Billy and I were excited, Missy was nervous, and without a captionist or interpreter, James had no way of knowing what Lee said from the platform.

I had a moment of panic when Lee walked toward

us after Sunday school. I hadn't told him that Missy signing with me was a secret, and I was afraid he'd spill the beans. My panic was groundless.

Lee told us good morning as he rushed past, his mind obviously on his Senior Sunday preparations.

During the church service, Billy sat with the other seniors at the front of the sanctuary. Normally, I would've sat at the front before I sang, but I didn't want to risk giving away the surprise by having Missy sit with me.

James was confused when I sat with the family, but Grandpa told him that he wanted all of us to sit together to see Billy honored. James accepted that explanation without question, and Grandpa winked conspiratorially at me when he wasn't looking.

During senior recognition, I did my best not to cry when they called Billy's name and announced his plans for the future. As he'd said that morning, he'd still be part of the family. Nothing could change that.

Despite my best efforts, Missy still had to fix my mascara with a tissue once it was over. After the congregation sang a couple more songs and the ushers collected the offering, it was the moment we'd been waiting for.

"Miss Kallyna Griffin and Miss Melissa Carver will now lead us in worship," Pastor Benjamin announced.

Wondering why the man refused to use nicknames, I got up, and Missy followed me to the front of the church. I forced myself not to look back and see the puzzled expression I knew James had on his face, but it was a near thing. When we reached the stage, I accepted the microphone from Pastor Benjamin and glanced at Missy. Seeing that she was ready, I nodded to the sound guy. As the intro music played, I looked out at the crowd.

Billy was grinning from his pew in the front row. Grandpa was gazing at me with pride in his eyes and a smile on his face. James was smiling too, though his eyes seemed to have an extra glimmer.

Then I turned my eyes away from the crowd and looked up toward the One I was truly singing for. When the intro ended, I closed my eyes and began to sing.

~March 31, 2019; 3:00 p.m.~

The door to the hospital room opens slowly. It's dim in the room because of the rain, but I can still easily see James come in. He has dark circles under his eyes and looks completely exhausted. Since he goes to school twelve hours away, he must have driven all night to get here this fast.

"I'm so glad you're here," I say and sign.

Then I walk into his waiting arms. He hugs me tight, and one knot in my stomach unclenches. I only see James during breaks and over the summer these days. I hate him being so far away, but I understand why God led him and Missy to where He did. The university they attend has a good ASL program, which is what they're both majoring in. Missy wants to become an interpreter, and James plans to go to seminary after he graduates and become a pastor for the deaf.

"How's Grandpa?" James asks, pulling away from me.

"The doctor is hopeful," I tell him, frowning as I try to remember how to sign that. Not having to sign as often, I'm very out of practice.

"The doctor is hopeful," James repeats, letting me know he understood. His speech reading has gotten better over the years.

Billy waves to get his attention and hands him a piece of paper that says 'The doctor was here an hour ago. He said that since Grandpa made it through the night, he thinks he'll recover.'

James reads it and turns to look at me. "Has he woken up since they brought him in?"

"A few times, but he's been pretty out of it," I say, suppressing a yawn.

James eyes me with concern. "You look exhausted, Ally."

"So do you," I say and sign. "How was the drive?"

"Long, but fine," he says.

I look up at him guiltily. "You didn't have to come. We would've been OK."

He rolls his eyes. "I wanted to be here. For Grandpa and for you." He glances between Billy and me, smiling sheepishly. "Besides, I've been needing an excuse to come down here so I can talk to Missy's mom without her knowing it."

"Why do you need to talk to Ms. Cathy?" I ask, frowning.

"Well, normally I'd ask her dad for his blessing, but since he's not in the picture..." He shrugs. "I figured I'd ask her mom instead."

My eyes widen, and I throw my arms around him again.

Billy stands up and slaps him on the back.

"Congratulations," we both tell him.

James grins and turns toward the bed. "Grandpa?"

I follow his gaze.

Grandpa's eyes are open, and he's looking at us, love shining from his eyes.

"We're here, Grandpa," I say, walking over to stand on his right. Billy's on his left, and James is at the foot of his bed, across from him. Just as we always are when we pray. We all smile down at him. *Please Lord*, I ask silently. *Please let Grandpa be OK.*

As I look at my cousins' faces, I can tell they're asking the Lord for the same thing. And somehow, despite my continued anxiety, I know that God is with us as we stand here, praying, and listening to the rain.

Thank you…

for purchasing this Watershed Books title. For other inspirational stories, please visit our on-line bookstore at www.pelicanbookgroup.com.

For questions or more information, contact us at customer@pelicanbookgroup.com.

Watershed Books
Make a Splash!™
an imprint of Pelican Book Group
www.PelicanBookGroup.com

Connect with Us
www.facebook.com/Pelicanbookgroup
www.twitter.com/pelicanbookgrp

To receive news and specials, subscribe to our bulletin
http://pelink.us/bulletin

May God's glory shine through
this inspirational work of fiction.

AMDG

You Can Help!

At Pelican Book Group it is our mission to entertain readers with fiction that uplifts the Gospel. It is our privilege to spend time with you awhile as you read our stories.

We believe you can help us to bring Christ into the lives of people across the globe. And you don't have to open your wallet or even leave your house!

Here are 3 simple things you can do to help us bring illuminating fiction™ to people everywhere.

1) If you enjoyed this book, write a positive review. Post it at online retailers and websites where readers gather. And share your review with us at reviews@pelicanbookgroup.com (this does give us permission to reprint your review in whole or in part.)

2) If you enjoyed this book, recommend it to a friend in person, at a book club or on social media.

3) If you have suggestions on how we can improve or expand our selection, let us know. We value your opinion. Use the contact form on our web site or e-mail us at customer@pelicanbookgroup.com

God Can Help!

Are you in need? The Almighty can do great things for you. Holy is His Name! He has mercy in every generation. He can lift up the lowly and accomplish all things. Reach out today.

Do not fear: I am with you; do not be anxious: I am your God. I will strengthen you, I will help you, I will uphold you with my victorious right hand.

~Isaiah 41:10 (NAB)

We pray daily, and we especially pray for everyone connected to Pelican Book Group—that includes you! If you have a specific need, we welcome the opportunity to pray for you. Share your needs or praise reports at http://pelink.us/pray4us

Free eBook Offer

We're looking for booklovers like you to partner with us! Join our team of influencers today and periodically receive free eBooks!

For more information
Visit http://pelicanbookgroup.com/booklovers

How About Free Audiobooks?

We're looking for audiobook lovers, too! Partner with us as an audiobook lover and periodically receive free audiobooks!

For more information
Visit
http://pelicanbookgroup.com/booklovers/freeaudio.html

or e-mail
booklovers@pelicanbookgroup.com